The Edge
of the Firelight

Gordon A. Bain

Cover illustration by Rick Nass, www.rnass.com

ISBN: 1478291257

ISBN-13: 978-1478291251

Contents

Acknowledgement

On a night at a scout campout a few years ago I was sitting back from the campfire reviewing the details of a story from a book. A couple of scouts looked over my shoulder and asked me what I was doing. They were shocked. They had assumed that I'd invented all the stories I'd told them to that point. With characteristic teenage subtlety, one of them said "What? You get your stories from books? Mr. Bain, that's really lame!" I took that as a challenge, and started work on *How Gordie Came to Castle Rock* the next weekend. That was the start of what has been a fun ride and has led to a lot of fun for me and for those who enjoy my stories.
Thanks for the push guys, and by the way, telling other people's stories isn't lame – it's just an easy way to get started.

I must also thank the scouts and leaders of Pack 549 and Troop 628 from Verona and Madison, WI. Thanks for the encouragement and for loving my stories. I would never have written them without your enthusiasm and support.
My thanks also go to my son, Justin, for being my excuse for being a scout leader, for inspiring the main character in *The Missing Bugler*, and for being a good sport about using his name in my stories.
Final thanks go to my wife, Rachel, for sorting out my lousy punctuation and for pointing out where I was using expressions that are "too British" and suggesting suitable American alternatives that will be more meaningful to this audience.

Disclaimer

Although some of these stories are set in real places, all of the stories themselves are fictional. As they were originally written and told they featured real people. I have changed those names for this book, or used only a first name or last initial in order to protect those individuals' online privacy. If you came across something in this book and think that you recognize a person in one of the stories, please remember that it's all made up. Nothing that you read here reflects actual actions by actual people.

Introduction

The stories in this book were written to be told to an audience of ten to fifteen year old boys. In this case the boys are a group of Boy Scouts from southern Wisconsin, but the stories could be told to almost any audience with only small modifications. There is a glossary at the end of the book with explanations of some abbreviations and scouting terms.

The great joy of telling a story in person is in being able to make a real connection with your audience. I have found that putting members of the audience, people they know, or places that they visit into the story really draws them into the story and helps them to connect to it and to remember it later. If you are reading this book with the intention of telling the stories in it to an audience of your own I encourage you to change the stories to help your audience to connect with you. Set them in your own neighborhood or your own favorite campgrounds. Put some kids from the audience in the story, but choose carefully – not every kid can deal with being eaten by a werewolf when over-tired after a day or more of outdoor activities! The kids will love it, and you'll be amazed at how the different personalities react to being a hero or a victim. Don't be afraid to send up the Scoutmaster, the Camp Director, or the Assistant Principle of their school. A few cheap shots about how gullible adults can be will go a long way too.

Find inspiration and stories where you can. When you tell stories, do it from memory and make them your own. Tell the story with feeling, give characters an accent if appropriate. Be loud, speak softly, pause for effect, move around as you talk – whatever it takes to add life and passion to the tale. Story-tellers continue a tradition of entertaining an adolescent audience at a campfire that goes back to or beyond the very beginnings of human civilization. There aren't many things you can do in the 21st century that have not changed in four thousand years. Enjoy reading these tales and most of all, have fun telling the story.

1 The Ghost of Wildcat Mountain

Walther Schoenfelder served his country with honor in World War I. On being discharged, he moved back to his home state, took three years of accumulated army pay, some money from his parents and a big bank loan, and bought himself 160 acres in a fertile valley backed by a tree-covered ridge. There, he began to farm.

Life was good. His first year's crops came in well, his animals were healthy and he had the good fortune to meet a pretty young woman named Louise at a church social. Walther and Louise married in July of 1920. They wasted no time in starting a family, and by 1933 they had five children, ages six to twelve. Now Walther and Louise were not rich by any means, but they had what they needed and lived comfortably enough – if you consider a four room log cabin with an outhouse and no indoor plumbing to be comfortable!

Each autumn Walther would go out into the woods at the back of his property to chop wood and hunt game to store to keep his family fed and warm for the winter. By the middle of October the crops would all be in and he was out in the woods every day. He hunted pheasant, turkey, deer and squirrel, all with a double-barreled shotgun. The game would be hung in a shed, then salted or smoked for storage through the winter.

By 1933 he was going out with his children when he went hunting. Game levels would vary from year to year, but the previous winter had been a mild one, and Walther had been expecting a lot of deer that year. Strangely, however, not many seemed to be coming into his hillside. The whole wood was just unnaturally quiet that year.

With seven mouths to feed and too little game for comfort in the smoke-house, as the day began to wane on October 17 Walther decided to do a game drive. He sent the kids up to the top of the ridge and had them fan out, then come down as *beaters* to drive the game toward him and his gun at the bottom of the hill. As the kids started to come down the hill, shouting and yelling, the yells of one, eight-year-old Lilly, changed to two short screams. The second scream was cut off sharply.

Dusk was falling, and as the light began to fail, Walther rushed up the hill and the other children converged on where Lilly had been. They found blood and a blood trail, and the children reported hearing growling and snarling just after Lilly screamed. They tried to follow the trail but lost it in the dark. They brought flaming torches and searched the best they could, but no further trace of Lilly could be found.

At daybreak Walther sent his two oldest to town to fetch men to help search. They found the blood trail and followed it for a mile, but then it simply disappeared. After searching all day, as the sun sank towards the horizon, one of the men looked up to sight the first stars and saw Lilly's body on a limb twenty feet up a tree.

On bringing the body down, they found that Lilly had been killed by some kind of animal. Her neck had been broken by a bite from behind, and her organs torn out and eaten. One of the men shone a new invention, a battery-powered flashlight, around in the woods as the dusk thickened and glimpsed a pair of eyes shining in the darkness. Another man fired a shot at the eyes and with a rustle of undergrowth, the eyes vanished.

For many days, the men of the county search the wood, but found no sign of what killed Lilly. On All Hallow's Eve, the search was called off and the serious business of hunting game began again. All the men had families who needed to be fed through the winter and in spite of all the search parties, the deer seem to be returning to the woods.

It took several months for the Schoenfelder family to find some kind of normalcy again after Lilly's death, but in those days it was pretty common for one or two of your kids to die of one thing or another during childhood, so they took it in stride and when the forested hill turned orange once more in the fall of 1934, Walther and his four remaining children went back out into the forest to hunt and gather wood.

On the night of October 17, they decided to have a campfire out there before heading back to the cabin for the night. All were tired and, being a year since Lilly's death, they were swapping stories of the good times they had had with her. Suddenly seven-year-old Max pitched forward into the firelight. It took a moment for Walther and the other children to realize what they were looking at. On Max's back was the biggest cat any of them had ever seen. It had him by the back of the neck, and every one of them heard the crunch as it bit down hard, smashing his spine, killing him with that single bite as he hung like a rag-doll in its maw.

The cat used that moment of confusion to leap out of the firelight, its prize still hanging from its jaws. Walther grabbed his shotgun and fired a shot at it. The buckshot caught the cat in the haunch, wounding but not killing it, and they heard the sound of the cat crashing through the undergrowth as it dragged poor Max's body away to be devoured.

The surviving Schoenfelders had all had a good look at the cat. Describing it to the sheriff and the men of the town the next day, all agreed that it must be a cougar, a mountain lion, a puma, a panther – all names for the same animal depending on where in the Americas it is found. Dogs were brought and they tracked the cat to the remains of Max's body – I'll spare you the description of its condition – and then on over hills and fields until, finally, the dogs caught up to the bleeding, weakened cat and forced it up a tree. The cougar was as angry and agitated as a big cat can get. As the men gathered round the tree, it hissed, spat and roared its defiance until Walther was found and took his revenge, firing both barrels into its snarling face in quick succession.

The cougar's body was hauled down to the fields by the farm and burned. They did not skin it or mount the ruined head. It was simply disposed of like another piece of trash. Four days later at the east end of the farm, as the rising run cast the shadows long, two dark lines spread behind two headstones. Max had been laid to rest next to his elder sister.

The rest of October and November was a time of mourning for Walther and Louise. Even with the killer cougar dead, Walther did not have the heart to venture into the woods in search of game. Fearing that the family would go hungry, other men of the town came over and began to hunt in Walther's woods, bringing the meat they shot back to the Schoenfelders for their winter stores.

The hunting stopped with the first snow when one of the men found tracks in the snow. They were the unmistakable tracks of a big cat. The tracks never went very far, however. They seemed to start with no warning and to end without trace. Saying nothing to Walther or his family, the men of the town left the woods and returned to their own families to make ready for the long winter.

The fall of 1935 was a tense time in the Schoenfelder home. The children were not keen to accompany their father into the forest. Even with the cougar dead, the woods behind the Schoenfelder home were a place of bad memories and a sense of threat and danger.

The oldest, Gustav, was now a tall lad of fourteen. He had been given an old army rifle by one of the old men of the town, and he stood guard over his brother and sister as they dragged logs and branches out of the woods to be cut up in the open, where nothing could sneak up on them. The tension grew with each day of fall. Each child knew that the chance of another cougar taking over the range of the dead one, and that it would consider them its prey, was small. With each rustle in the undergrowth, however, all would stop and look and the rifle would be brought to bear on the sound.

And so it was, on the evening of October 16, that as they were finishing up their sawing and chopping for the night, Gustav shone his light across the edge of the woods and picked out a pair of eyes, watching them. Passing his flashlight to his sister Meg, he clearly saw the silhouette of a cougar standing at the edge of the woods. Cool as can be, Gustav raised his rifle, aimed just behind the cat's shoulder and fired. **BANG!** He would always swear that it was a perfect shot, but the bullet simply shook a bush behind the cougar, and it turned its gaze on him with horrible intensity, opened its mouth in a silent snarl, and limped.....yes, limped, off into the woods.

That night the family sat quietly in their cabin with the door and windows barred. Could *another* cougar truly have come to torment them? After an uneasy night's sleep, they went back out to the woods in full daylight to look for tracks or a blood trail. They found no blood, just one huge paw-print in some soft mud. After spending the morning combing the woods together with their guns, Walther and Gustav declared it safe, and the family returned to its work of cutting, splitting and stacking wood for the winter.

As the light began to fail, they withdrew to the split-rail fenced paddock around their cabin and began to shine lights on the woods.

It was October 17th, the anniversary of the two attacks that cost them two of their children. There, again, on the edge of the woods, was a pair of shining eyes.

All lights were turned on the spot where the eyes stood. Dimly lit, but clear to see, stood a full grown cougar. Dropping low into a stalking crouch, it came toward the Schoenfelder family one pace at a time. Walther fired first – **BOOM!!** – a special load he had prepared just for this occasion. His shot was followed by the crack of Gustav's rifle. But the shots seemed to pass right through the slowly advancing cat. Quickly, Gustav worked the bolt and – **CRACK!** – fired again, but to no effect. The cougar quickened its pace.

A cougar can leap 45 feet from a still start, 60 if it has a run, and that is what this one did. It leapt over the fence and smashed into nine year old Meg with the full force of its 180 pounds. Meg saw it coming, raised her arms and screamed – once in fear and a second time as the cats jaws came down on her arm.

Gustav spun to fire the rifle as best he could – if you've ever tried to turn and aim a 303 rifle in close quarters you'll understand that it's no small thing – and fired. There was no doubting it now. His bullet passed straight through the cougar as if it wasn't even there, splintering a fence post behind it.

As Gustav struggled to work a new round into the chamber, the cougar turned on him and with another silent snarl, leapt into his chest, knocking him to the ground, sending the rifle flying and sinking its claws into his flesh.

Walther with his gun and Louise with an axe both tried to beat the animal away, but their weapons passed through the ghostly form and had no effect. The cougar, however, simply stood with its front paws on the still form of Gustav and stared at Walther. It made no sound as it bunched its muscles to attack, then pounced at Walther, passed straight through him, and disappeared.

Gustav and Meg both had claw wounds and Meg had some deep bites on her arm. Both were taken to the hospital in the state capital for treatment and, although Gustav's wounds turned septic, with the help of the new penicillin drugs, both kids returned to health after a couple of weeks.

The story of the ghost cougar of Vernon County spread fast, and on Thanksgiving Day, 1935, an article appeared in the Sentinel newspaper under the headline "Ghost Cougar Terrorizes Family". By the first of December, it seemed that every hunter, glory seeker and wacko in the state, licensed or otherwise, was roaming the woods behind the Schoenfelder property at dusk.

A few of them found paw prints in the snow, but they always seemed to appear out of nowhere and disappear without trace.

1936 was a good year on the farm. Summer weather was perfect, the farm animals were fat and the crops set records. If it had not been for the Sentinel running an anniversary piece "Will Ghost Cougar Return???" on October 7, the fall might have been perfect.

As the fateful weekend approached, the woods were packed with city hunters, and countless skunks, badgers, raccoons, deer, two lost sheep and one unfortunate cow all fell victim to a culture of "if it moves in the woods, shoot!" The county sheriff decided that if the hundreds of hunters roaming the woods got any jumpier, they were going to start shooting each other, and he and his team of deputies began ticketing anyone with a gun and no valid game license. The city folks headed home in a steady flow, and by October 17, only a few dozen dedicated souls roamed the woods with flashlights and rifles.

It was on that night, of course, that the cat came back. Before the night was over, no less than a dozen hunters had been attacked. None was killed, but all were knocked down, clawed or bitten. Each one told the same tale of a ghostly cougar that came out of nowhere and without a sound. Bullets and shot passed right through it, and it seemed to have appetite only to attack, not to eat.

The Schoenfelders were not there to see it. They had gone to the city for the week, where they slept in a building of stone behind a door of stoutest oak, far from the woods and ghost that haunted them.

You might think that this would be the end of the story, but in a sense, it is only the beginning. The cougar was not seen again all winter, but each year it would reappear, just as reliable as can be, on the night of October 17. Each year for two weeks leading up to Halloween, its ghostly form would be seen pacing the edge of the woods at dusk. A few brave souls would see the reflection of its eyes as they shone their lights at the woods from the safety of the Schoenfelders' cabin. Walther and Louise made good money charging people to spend those nights in their cabin, while they decamped to the city. In 1939, they made the move to the city for good, with Walther taking a job as a carpenter and the whole family turning its back on the farm and both the joys and the horrors they had suffered there.

War broke out in 1939 and America joined it in 1941. Gustav and his younger brother William joined up but Walther was considered too old. When it was all over, Gustav, who had fought bravely against both the cougar and the Japanese, had fallen on Saipan. William had survived without injury, but he had seen the world and wanted no more part of farm life in Wisconsin.

On the Schoenfelder farm, the eyes still shone from the woods in the night each October for two weeks before Halloween, and the place had too many memories of grief and struggle for Walther and his wife to bear. So, in the spring of 1947, they sold their property to the State of Wisconsin for use as part of a state park.

The director of the DNR asked Walther Schoenfelder to suggest a name for the new park that would encompass all his land and more. Walther looked back at him for a moment with an expression of sadness and.....something more. After a long pause, he replied "Wild Cat Mountain".

2 The Shade

Hayden had been enjoying the sixth grade, right up until the end of October. That was when his big sister, fifteen-year-old Megan, had fallen ill.

The illness had come on suddenly. Megan had been working on a project for her ninth-grade history class. It was something to do with looking up details of the lives of the first settlers of this area. She had started out by cataloging the information from the oldest headstones in the local graveyard. She cross-referenced these names to the property records at the Town Hall, then tracked down and interviewed some of the descendants to see what they could tell her about their ancestors. She even spent the night at one of the farms. Finally, she read all the books on local history at the city library. She had become ill at about the point that she finished interviewing people.

Megan had kept on working on her project and going to school, but she seemed to get weaker and more tired every day. Two weeks after the interviews, she had finished and turned in her project, but rather than giving her a boost, the end of the project seemed to drain the last of the life from her. She died in her sleep the night after she submitted the assignment.

The doctors weren't been able to figure out a cause of death. They said it was as if Megan's body had simply given up the spirit of life. All her organs had just steadily shut down until they gave out completely.

Megan's death had changed everything for Hayden. His parents were not dealing with it well. They barely spoke to him or to each other. Hayden didn't know how he was dealing with it. How do you assess something like that? One thing he did know, however. People don't just die for no reason. Megan became ill when she started researching that paper, and Hayden decided that he was going to find out if there was a connection.

Hayden started by reading the paper Megan had written. Most of it was what you'd expect. Families had come from "the old country", wherever that might have been, purchased land and settled down to farm. They had about a dozen kids each, two-thirds of whom survived to adulthood. Farms got divided among the kids when the first generation died. A bunch of the men went off to fight in the civil war. Some of them returned. Some didn't.

BUT there was one family, the Hendricksons, whose story was markedly different. Three brothers and a sister had come from Denmark, each starting a family on neighboring farms south of town. The farms were built around a deep central well from which they all drew their water. Each family had the usual six or ten kids, but only one child in each family survived to adulthood. The others would die, either of childhood diseases as young children or, with troubling regularity, at the age of fifteen.

With only one heir in each family, it was always the case that each Hendrickson farm passed undivided to the next generation. For generations it had been that way. To this day, the four farms, just two miles south of town, stood together around the old well and were farmed by descendants of the original owners.

As Hayden looked through his sister's notes he found that of the families who lived there now, two had one adult child each, one had a single son in elementary school, and one had two kids. One of those kids was his classmate Reid. Reid was a good guy, and looking at the history of his family, his chances of making it to his sixteenth birthday suddenly looked like exactly fifty percent.

This was worse than Hayden had thought. It was looking a lot like the Hendricksons or their land was under some sort of curse. Maybe that curse had struck down his sister, and maybe it aimed squarely at one of his friends too. And what about Hayden himself? Once a family had been struck by the curse once, would it stick forever? Would all but one of Hayden's children die before reaching sixteen? Worse yet, what might happen to Hayden if his parents had another baby!?

Hayden resolved to go straight to his best source for information. Reid was a Hendrickson and he lived on one of those farms. He had to know something.

Hayden positioned himself in front of Reid in the lunch line the next day, and when their trays were filled he suggested to Reid that the two of them go to an open table. Reid said, "Sure," and the two of them went off to a corner of the commons.

At first, neither of them said anything as they were digging into their food, but after a couple of minutes Reid broke the silence with, "I'm really sorry about your sister."

Hayden shrugged. "Thanks," he said. "I guess your family knows a lot about losing family members."

Reid looked puzzled by that. "What do you mean?" he asked.

"My sister interviewed some of the adults in your family for the project she was working on before... before she died," replied Hayden. "I don't quite know how to put it, but your family has a pretty high mortality rate."

"What are you talking about?" Reid asked. He looked like he was getting a bit upset. "Nobody but the real old folks in my family has died in my lifetime. We're not that big of a family anyway. My little brother and I are the only ones in two generations who aren't only children."

"That's just the point." Hayden leaned in closer to Reid and dropped his voice. "My sister found out that in the first few generations of your family to live in the States, all the kids but one would die before reaching adulthood."

Reid sat back and put down his fork. "Dude, I'm really sorry about your sister, but you're getting pretty weird here. Maybe you need to see a shrink or something." With that, he stood up, picked up his tray, walked over to another table of sixth-graders and sat down to finish his meal.

Hayden finished his lunch alone.

The next day after lunch, Reid walked right up to Hayden and said, "We need to talk after school." Hayden rather hoped that Reid wasn't planning to try to beat him up. *At least*, he reflected, *I know for sure that the guy doesn't have a mean big brother.*

After they collected their backpacks and jackets from their lockers, Reid and Hayden went to a corner of the playground and sat down in the wood chips. "I'm sorry for getting weird on you yesterday," Hayden began.

Reid cut him off right away. "I talked to my great uncle and an aunt on the other farms last night. Everything you said is true. Nobody in my family has more than one kid any more. They all say that it sort of became a family tradition for exactly the reason you said. Anyone who had more than one kid ended up with only one in the end."

"Do they have any idea why?"

"Yeah, but you'd never believe me if I told you what they said. You'll have to see it for yourself."

"When?"

"How soon are you expected home from school?"

"My parents won't be home until 5:00. If I leave a message on the answering machine telling them where I am I don't have to be home until 5:30."

Reid produced a cell phone. "Tell them you're going to my house. We have newly hatched chickens that I can show you. They're funny, but cool to look at, and it's a legit excuse that any parent would buy."

They rode their bikes to the Hendrickson farms and dropped their back-packs in Reid's family kitchen. His mom was there and offered drinks and cookies, which the boys gratefully accepted. Then they went out to the barn where Reid did indeed have newly hatched chickens in an incubator.

"So, what did you want to show me?" Hayden asked.

"The inscription on the well," replied Reid.

The boys walked over to the old well that stood at the center where the back yards of the four farms met. There was a low machine shed next to it, with the sound of an electric pump coming from it.

"Somebody put in the electric pump back in the 1930s. Nobody's actually drawn water from the stone well since then, unless maybe they had to during a long power cut."

Reid led Hayden to the far side of the old stone well. "Here's what I wanted to show you."

He pointed at a piece of flat sandstone laid into the field-stone and cement construction of the well. Engraved into the sandstone for all to see was this inscription:

In the dark it will arrive.
Hope and pray that you'll survive.
For when the bells of midnight toll,
The Shade will come to reap your soul.

"Well, that's certainly an inspiring message!" said Hayden.

"Don't read it out loud," said Reid. "Nobody in my family does. They say it's bad luck."

"Did my sister read it out loud?"

"She might have. I wasn't there when she spoke to the old folks."

"She stayed the night. There was a tornado warning that evening, and she was already late because she had talked with so many people for so long. She called my parents and said that your parents had offered to let her sleep on the couch so that nobody had to go out in the risky weather to fetch her."

Reid thought for a moment. "I suppose she could have gone out at night. We all sleep upstairs, so no one would have heard her sneak out."

The boys contemplated this for a moment. Had Megan really snuck out on that stormy night to see what happened at the stroke of midnight?

Reid broke the silence. "You'd better get on home. I'll talk to my great uncle after dinner. He's the oldest one in the family. Megan talked with him the longest. If anyone knows more about the inscription, it'll be him."

So Hayden rode his bike back into town while Reid had his meal, then pulled on his boots and stomped across the farmyard to his great uncle's house.

Hayden's phone buzzed at about ten o'clock. It was a text message from Reid. "Be at school twenty mins early. Lots to tell."

Reid was already there when Hayden arrived at the bike rack to lock up his bike. "I got the whole story," he said.

As his great uncle told it, everything that Megan had found out about all but one kid dying before reaching sixteen was true. Around 1900, one of the families had only one child, a boy. The mother died in childbirth and the father never remarried. The other families had all worried that this line of the family would die out if the child succumbed, as so many of the Hendrickson children did, but he had survived every illness, hardship and injury to carry on his line. After that, other families on the farmsteads tried having only one child. In each case, the child would live. Any families that had more than one would see the children die until only one remained.

Reid's parents were the first ones since 1950 to have a second child. The old people had cautioned them not to, but Reid's parents said that it was all just nonsense, and with modern medicine pretty much any child who got sick could be cured. Reid's great uncle said that he had not planned to discuss this with Reid until he was older, so as not to scare him, but since Reid was asking and already knew enough to scare himself, he told him what he knew, and added this piece of advice. "Never, never, go out to the well at midnight."

"Are you scared?" Hayden asked Reid.

"Nah, it's just a superstitious old man telling tales. My mom and dad are right."

"Even after what happened to Megan?"

Reid shook his head "no" and said, "Hayden, do you want to come for a sleepover on Friday? We'll sneak out at midnight and see what this is all about."

Hayden thought about this for a minute. "I'm an only child now. You're not, and you're a Hendrickson. How about we set up my iPod as a video camera and I'll go out there. We'll take all the protective measures we can, and you can watch the film in the morning, whatever happens to me."

Reid looked at Hayden and spoke his words back to him, "Even after what happened to Megan?"

Hayden stood up straight, squared his shoulders and set his jaw. "Yeah, I need to know. Plus, maybe I have a score to settle."

In library that day, Reid and Hayden spent the entire fifty minutes in the fantasy section paging through books with spirits and creatures of the night, looking for ways to fight or repel them. After school, they biked over to the city library and hit the encyclopedias and the internet for more information. The next day, Thursday, Reid went to the grocery store on his way home and Hayden went to the hardware store.

At five o'clock on Friday, Hayden's dad dropped him off at Reid's house. They carried everything that Hayden had brought into a corner of the barn and laid it out alongside the things that Reid pulled out of a plastic tote that had been hidden under some hay. Here is what they had:

- Three wooden stakes, each four feet long
- One sheath knife with a six inch blade
- Twenty bulbs of garlic
- Four large containers of garlic salt
- One 20lb bag of softener salt
- One small pot of metallic silver paint
- Ten rounds of nine-millimeter ammunition
- One Beretta pistol
- One wooden crucifix about ten inches tall
- Fifty feet of string
- One roll of duct tape

Hayden stared at the pistol. "Reid, is that real? Where did you get it?"

"It's my dad's. He thinks I don't know where he keeps it. Adults can be pretty dense sometimes. You keep your mouth shut about it, though. If he ever found out that I'd taken it he'd skin me alive."

Hayden couldn't take his eyes off the gun. "Is it loaded?"

"Not yet, stupid," Reid replied. "Don't you know that you never store a gun loaded? Weren't you listening when we did rifle Merit Badge in Scouts? Maybe you shouldn't have the gun tonight!"

"Oh no! I want it," said Hayden.

The preparations continued. They painted the tips of the bullets with the silver metallic paint. They weren't real silver bullets, but were as close as they could get, and close enough to ruin a monster's night, they hoped. Reid used the knife to sharpen the stakes to wicked points. "Remember," he told Hayden, "aim for the heart."

The crucifix was also painted silver, then tied to a length of string so that it could hang around Hayden's neck. Ten of the big garlic bulbs were threaded onto some more string. This was also set up to go around Hayden's neck. They threaded individual small cloves from the other ten garlic bulbs onto the string to make a 15 foot line of garlic. Both boys stank of garlic after that, and got some really strange looks from Reid's parents at dinner time. Nobody objected when the boys asked if they could take their food up to Reid's room to eat.

After dinner, they headed out into the falling dusk and fetched everything out of the barn and over to the pump-house by the well. The iPod, fully charged, was duct-taped to the side of the pump-house.

The long garlic string was laid out in a circle around where Hayden was to wait. Outside the garlic they laid a continuous line of salt crystals. Next to the place where Hayden was to stand they stacked the three stakes and the tote with the crucifix, the pistol and the magazine in it. A second, smaller circle of garlic salt was laid, as a last resort, close in by where Hayden was to stand. If garlic and salt each repelled monsters on their own, garlic salt had to be twice as good!

Afraid that Reid's parents would come to look at what they were doing, the boys went inside at 8:30 p.m. They played video games until ten when Reid's parents told them to get ready for bed, then talked until a little after eleven, twice being told to quiet down and go to sleep. It was important to behave completely normally, so as not to arouse suspicion. Quiet they may have been, but asleep they were most certainly not. Every ten minutes, one of the boys would get up and look out of the window, where the well in the farmyard was illuminated by a half moon in an inky black sky.

At quarter to midnight, Hayden and Reid slipped out of bed. Hayden got his sweater on, then they tip-toed down the stairs to the kitchen door. There, Hayden put on his sneakers and a stocking cap, turned around to face Reid and shook his hand.

"Don't stick the gun in your belt," Reid whispered. "If it goes off there you'll be the only boy singing soprano in the high school choir."

Hayden couldn't help but laugh at this. "Thanks buddy. I'll try to remember that."

Reid closed the door behind Hayden then crept back upstairs to watch from his bedroom window. Hayden walked out to his circle of protection by the pump-house, turned on the iPod camera, and waited. It was five minutes before midnight.

As the moments passed, Hayden became conscious of his heart pounding harder and faster. He pushed the button on his watch for the light. 11:58. He opened the tote, pulled out the crucifix and the string of ten whole cloves of garlic, and hung both around his neck. He picked up the Beretta and the magazine, pushed the magazine home, and checked his watch. 11:59. He pulled back the slide and released it to chamber a round, then turned the safety catch to *fire* and set the pistol down next him on the low cover of the pump-house. Check time: Midnight. Somewhere in the distance Hayden heard a church bell ringing out.

It was perfectly quiet in the farmyard. Hayden's eyes were well adjusted to the moonlight, and he was watching the well intently. With no sound at all, the well simply disappeared. It was as if it had been swallowed by the night. Where a moment ago there had been an old stone well, there was now a gap in the night. It was a darkness so perfect that no light passed through it and none escaped it. That, Hayden thought, as he gripped the crucifix in one hand and a stake in the other, must be *the Shade*.

The darkness approached Hayden, silhouetted now against the white-washed wall of one of the other farmhouses. It was no longer a shapeless form, but looked more like a cloak with a hood. There were neither arms nor legs but there was clearly a head atop the body. The Shade swept slowly across the ground between the well and Hayden, stopping just outside the line of salt.

"Don't come any closer!" Hayden said. He had intended it as bold shout, but somehow it seemed to come out as little more than a scared whisper.

The Shade appeared to be watching Hayden. It floated there, not ten feet away from him for what seemed like an eternity. Then, slowly, it drifted across the line of salt toward him. On it drifted, over the line of garlic, all the way up to the line of garlic salt, no more than two feet from Hayden's face, where it stopped.

To Hayden, looking at the Shade was like looking into *nothingness* he couldn't see through it, but he couldn't see it either. It was just there, silent, menacing, watching him. Hayden held the crucifix up between his chest and the Shade and drew back his arm with the stake. "Stay away from me!" he said, a little louder this time.

The Shade did not react. It just kept on floating there. Hayden began to get a little control of himself. "Are you what killed my sister?" he asked.

The answer, when it came, seemed not to come from the Shade, but from every direction *except* the Shade. "Yeeeessssssss," it said.

Hayden took aim at where he thought a man's heart would be relative to the head if the Shade were a man and threw the stake in his hand. The stake vanished. The Shade did not move. Hayden picked up a second stake and poked at the Shade, trying to stab it again and again. No effect. The stake seemed to vanish as it touched the Shade, and to reappear when he pulled it back. Hayden dropped the stake and reached for the Beretta, his last weapon.

Quick as a flash, the Shade flew towards Hayden. Before he could bring the gun to bear, the Shade passed *through* Hayden's body, leaving him with the feeling of having all the warmth sucked out of him. He staggered at the shock of it, nearly falling but keeping his feet. He turned to look where the shade had gone and saw it now silhouetted against Reid's house, again floating some three feet from where he stood. "What have you done to me?" Hayden asked it.

Once again, it seemed that the air all around answered, with no sound coming from the Shade.

The line's last heir,
His soul I'll spare.
He'll not be harmed,
His life is charmed.

The shade began to drift slowly towards Reid's house. Hayden's hand tightened around the hilt of the pistol. It was heavy, and the chill of the Shade passing through him made Hayden feel weak, but he stepped out of his useless circle of no protection at all and ran to catch up with the Shade so that Reid's house was no longer behind it. Hayden raised the gun like he'd seen actors do in cop shows and squeezed the trigger.

BANG!

In the stillness of the night the pistol sounded like a canon. The recoil made Hayden's arms hurt, as did holding the heavy pistol at arm's length. The Shade stopped. Had the silver bullet actually had an effect on it?

BANG! BANG! BANG! He fired three more shots that echoed back and forth between the farmhouses.

Lights began to come on in all the houses. A dog barked in one. The shade drifted towards Hayden slightly then stopped. Once more the cold voice spoke from the air around Hayden.

With bravery for friend you've fought
And so this night his soul you've bought.
But let all those who call this home,
Remember words inscribed in stone.
For when the bells of midnight toll,
The Shade will come to reap your soul.

The final word "soul" seemed to hang in the air as the Shade flew through the air and vanished back into the well.

As Hayden gathered his senses, he realized that the recoil of the gun had knocked him onto his butt in the dirt of the farmyard. He lowered the gun, prised the fingers of his right hand off the grip where they seemed to have frozen around it, and pushed the safety catch back to *safe*.

Reid got to Hayden at exactly the same time as his aunt's chocolate lab, with the result that all three of them ended up in a tangled pile of arms, legs, paws and drool. Reid's dad and a couple of uncles got there next with flashlights. They picked up the Beretta and the boys, and led them both firmly by the arm back to Reid's kitchen.

Hayden and Reid tried their best to explain the whole story, but Reid's mom and dad kept interrupting so it wasn't easy. His parents were pretty much focused on the fact that the boys had the gun and were shooting at shadows in the night. And did Hayden's parents realize just how messed up he was from his sister's death to be doing something like this? He'd always seemed like such a sensible boy before! As for Reid, he was lucky that nobody had gotten hurt through his foolishness in taking his father's gun. At least, his dad added with a meaningful look at Reid, nobody had gotten hurt...yet.

The boys were put to bed in separate rooms, and the chocolate lab was put to bed in the kitchen so that there'd be an alert if they tried to sneak out for any more funny business.

In the morning, Hayden retrieved his iPod from the pump-house wall. The battery was dead so they couldn't look at the video right away. Reid's mom called Hayden's parents to come and get him, told the story from their point of view, and sent Hayden home to the tune of another lecture on how kids shouldn't play with guns, and what the heck was he thinking? And didn't they teach him better than that? And didn't he learn about proper gun safety in Boy Scouts as well?

Apparently Reid's and Hayden's parents talked on Sunday, because when they compared notes at school on Monday the boys found that they had been dealt more or less identical punishments. Both were grounded for two weeks. No TV. No iPod. No video games. No computer unless for school assignments. All free time beyond what was required to do homework to be filled with extra chores. As Reid pointed out, Hayden could be grateful that his family did not keep animals. Reid's mom had apparently also made his dad get rid of the Beretta, so his dad was doubly ticked off at him about that.

The two weeks of punishment seemed to last forever, but when they did finally end the boys got together in Hayden's room on Saturday afternoon to look at the video from the iPod. The picture was grainy because it had been so dark, but you could clearly see the Shade as a blackness more perfect than all the rest, all the way to the point where it passed through Hayden and went out of the frame. And you could hear its voice as a whisper on the recording when it spoke to Hayden. A blacker black on blackness and a whispery voice is not the sort of thing that convinces skeptical adults, however, so they decided to keep it to themselves.

What did it mean when it said, "His soul you've bought," they wondered? Did it mean that Hayden facing down the Shade was the price of both Reid and his little brother being allowed to live? Did it mean only that the Shade would take no souls that night? Or did it mean that Reid's little brother was condemned to die? Its repeat of the words from the inscription on the well before it fled seemed to indicate that the curse had not been broken.

Whatever it meant, Reid's mom (who had married into the Hendrickson family) was sure that she was not going to live with that inscription on the well if it was going to drive her sons to run around shooting at ghosts in the night. Three days after Hayden and Reid's little adventure, she "accidentally" backed a tractor into the wall of the well, collapsing the whole stone structure into the shaft of the well. The rubble had totaled the piping for the electric pump, and the families had been forced to abandon the well and have a new, completely modern well bored over a hundred yards from the nearest livestock pen in order to meet 21st century building standards. That meant that the well-head was now about three hundred yards from the nearest farmhouse. Reid's great uncle had finished the job of demolishing the old well-head, filling up the shaft with rubble and dirt, and removing the pump and pump-house.

All that stands on that spot today is a dog house. The dog who lives there is not chained, and is very fond of Reid and his brother. She has the nose of a bloodhound, the eyes of a cat, hearing like no creature you've ever met and a growl that would curdle your blood. Anything that comes looking for one of the Hendrickson kids will have to get past her first.

Did any or all of these measures save Reid and his brother or put an end to the curse and the Shade? Only time will tell the outcome of <u>that</u> story.

3   Stargazing Under a Full Moon

Notes to the story teller:

This story was written to include real people in the troop. The boys love it when they are put into the story. If you want to do the same when you tell it, the following is a description of 'the cast'. Fill it with your own scouts and leaders as you please!

Mr. Thorpe	A scoutmaster or assistant scoutmaster who is bald, or noticeably balding
David Stern	The ASM best able to take a joke
Ben	A blonde scout
Jake	A blonde scout
Nick	A confident scout who can stand being teased a little; it helps if he has a little brother who at least one of the scouts knows
Patrick	Nick's brother
Sam	A quiet kid who you wouldn't really expect to be cast as the hero
Tanner	Sam's usual tent-buddy
Alan and Justin	Two scouts who are basically low profile guys who get on with things without drawing much

	attention to themselves
Alec, Anthony and Eddie	The three oldest scouts present
David	The scout who has the most trouble waking up in the morning
Zack	A college age ASM or recent "graduate" of the troop who is popular with the boys
Ross and Lawrence	The two nerdiest kids in the troop

Stargazing Under a Full Moon

Troop 268 was one of the most successful scout troops in Madison, Wisconsin. As any scout parent will tell you, one of the keys to a successful troop is a good scoutmaster. He should be a man of good character, of course, and it helps immensely if he's a real *character* as well. Troop 268's scoutmaster was a man who epitomized both these characteristics. Tall, friendly, honest, only moderately over-weight, not *too* unfit, and as bald as can be, Mr. Thorpe was definitely a hit with his boys.

The February campout in Wisconsin can be a challenge, winter weather being what it is. This winter was one of the snowiest on record, and the air was crisp as the scouts burrowed into a snow bank, making a whole row of snow caves to sleep in. Mr. Thorpe looked over at them occasionally as he dug out his own cave. He sighed as he considered that he was condemned to spend the coming two nights in a closed space with David

Stern, one of his ASMs who was notorious for the volume of both his snoring and his flatulence. Mr. Stern was inside the cave now, hollowing it out and making benches on each side for them to sleep on.

There had been a fresh snowfall the night before. There wasn't much accumulation, only half an inch or so, but it was over a well frozen snowpack and was perfect for seeing animal prints. Of course, around the snow caves there were now no prints to be seen except those of snow boots in sizes five through twelve, but stepping away from the devastation of the scout encampment, Mr. Thorpe found beautiful tracks in the snow.

Back at the camp Mr. Thorpe found that the patrol leaders had set up a couple of stoves and were heating water for hot chocolate and getting cookies ready for cracker barrel. They had a campfire built to warm them too, and were gathering around it and beginning to tell jokes and stories for a campfire program. It would be a short one tonight, Thorpe reckoned. The sky was crystal clear, the sun had gone just gone down and the temperature was dropping fast.

Thorpe had agreed to take three of the boys who were working on their astronomy merit badge out onto the frozen lake to look at the stars. It was both a blessing and pity that there was a full moon tonight, he reflected. A blessing because they would have no trouble finding their way around, and a pity because there would be a large chunk of sky where they couldn't see the stars next to the moon's bright circle.

Thorpe took the senior patrol leader aside before letting the boys go to bed, and between them they did a quick check of each cave, making sure that they were set up properly. None of *his* boys would be going home with frost-bitten fingers or toes.

Of that much he would make certain. With a final lecture about the importance of changing into fresh, dry clothes for sleep, he packed all but his three aspiring astronomers off to bed.

The moon was already well up in the sky as the scoutmaster and three scouts trudged out onto the ice to get a clear view of the heavens. It cast clear moon-shadows across the snow from each tree and grass stalk. Suddenly a long, mournful note broke the stillness of the night. A howl that seemed filled with pain and heartbreak echoed across the lake.

"Now *that* didn't sound like a coyote at all!" thought Thorpe. That sounded just like the wolves he'd seen and heard in documentaries about the packs re-introduced to Yellowstone National Park. There are wolves in Wisconsin, but he'd never heard of one this far south. Could it really be?

"Look! Over there to the west," said one of the scouts, pointing at a shape by the lakeshore. Sure enough, there was the pyramidal shape of a wolf sitting on its haunches and raising its head to howl at the moon. As the four of them stared at it, the animal got up, stared at them for a moment, then loped off over a rise and vanished.

"That was **so** cool," said another scout. Mr. Thorpe agreed with him, but they were out there to look at stars, so he took out his electronic star scope and four star maps, one for each of them. For four or five minutes they searched for constellations before the sharp-eyed scout who had spotted the wolf first pointed to the north and in a hushed voice said, "Look, there he is again."

Sure enough, there on the ice, silhouetted against the white snow behind it, was the black form of the wolf, closer now than it had been before. Seeing them all looking at it, the wolf loped off to the east, vanishing in the reeds at the edge of the ice.

All that was left for the evening was to find Mars and Jupiter, so Mr. Thorpe turned to that topic next. It only took a couple of minutes and then it was time to go. The scouts passed their charts back to Mr. Thorpe and when he looked up from his pack he found the three scouts staring, transfixed, at the form of the wolf. Now it was standing to their east, scarcely a hundred yards away, watching them intently.

"It's like he's following us," whispered one of the scouts.

"No, he's not following us," said the oldest. "He's hunting us."

Those words were like pulling a trigger. The wolf burst into a run and came straight at the group. "Stay together!" yelled Thorpe.

A wolf's classic tactic is to spook a group into running so that he can identify the slowest or weakest and then take that animal down as the easiest target. Running away would play to that tactic, Thorpe knew, so instead he stepped in front of the three scouts, fixed his eyes on the wolf's and roared at it at the top of his voice. The wolf wasn't expecting this. He tried to stop his charge, but on the frozen lake he couldn't get the traction he needed and instead slipped on the ice and barreled, snarling, into Mr. Thorpe. Thorpe went down as the out-of-control wolf crashed into him. He tried to punch at it, but as he did so, the wolf whipped its head around and gashed Thorpe's right hand with his teeth. Thorpe landed a solid left hook on the animal's snout and it yelped in pain. Coming apart for a moment, both the wolf and Mr. Thorpe got to their feet. The scouts were yelling in panic and fear, but they did as they had been told and didn't scatter. The wolf took off running to the west again, heading for the shore where it had first been spotted.

Thorpe didn't wait to see where it stopped or went. "Together. Back to camp. Run!" he said. And together they ran, Thorpe cradling his bleeding right hand in his left mitten.

Back at the camp they roused Mr. Stern and re-built the fire. First they iced Thorpe's right hand, then they cleaned the wound as best they could by flashlight, and bandaged it up. Stern was all for taking Thorpe to the hospital right away, but Thorpe couldn't drive with his wounded hand, and if Stern drove him, that would leave the scouts without an adult leader. Since they couldn't fit all the scouts into either man's vehicle, they decided to wait until the morning, call for a couple of other troop adults to relieve them, and then take Thorpe for treatment. "After all", he remarked, "it's not like I'm going to go into shock. I'm too darned angry, and I just got to see a real, live wolf. Up close, and very, very personal!"

It was a long night for Mr. Thorpe. Pain killers can only do so much and his hand hurt more than it seemed like it ought to for that kind of wound. He awoke at first light feeling terribly tired. Stern was up too, and they immediately called the troop committee chair from one of their cell phones to tell him what had happened. The troop CC did better than just riding to the rescue. He called the county sheriff and in less than twenty minutes, two deputies showed up in Suburbans. One of them took Mr. Thorpe to the hospital while the other stayed and took statements from the boys and Mr. Stern. As the deputy was wrapping up, a cavalcade of vehicles pulled into the campground. It was the scouts' parents, the council Scout Executive and, inevitably, a TV station van.

The scouts got to tell their story to the Scout Executive who then gave an account of the calmness and heroism of the scouts and their leader to the TV people before ushering all the scouts into their parents' cars and out of the camp.

Thorpe took two weeks off work to get over his wound. It seemed to heal very quickly, really. The odd thing was, he wasn't doing any exercise while he recovered and yet, he felt fitter than he had in years.

During his recovery, Thorpe had also stayed away from weekly Tuesday night troop meetings. He'd heard that the Channel 15 TV crew showed up and wanted to interview people the week after the attack, and he just didn't need that, so he stayed away the second week too. At the first troop meeting back, he got a standing ovation when he stood up to do scoutmaster's announcements.

Not everything was entirely normal with Mr. Thorpe, however. One of the scouts saw him at Culver's ordering his burger rare, which was odd for a guy who always insisted that they cook their meat until it was almost black when they camped. Thorpe had taken up running too. One of the scouts was a cross-country runner who did several miles each morning, and he kept passing Thorpe on the street.

Come the March tent camp, which fell four weeks to the day after the February one, Mr. Thorpe looked a little rough on the Saturday morning. He brushed off questions about whether he was ill, saying that he'd slept badly but was otherwise okay. He didn't eat much breakfast, though.

That morning, the group went on a hike across ground still covered with a thin layer of snow. Ben was in the lead and found coyote tracks that he chose to follow. The tracks led to a deer that had been killed by something, presumably the coyote. The animal had had its throat ripped out and there was blood all over the ground. It was gruesome, but the boys all thought it was pretty cool, too.

Saturday night was another full moon, of course. Nick, Ben and Jake decided to sneak out for a bit of late night "writing your name in the snow". As they set about their work, Nick spotted a wolf watching them from about fifty feet away. The moment that Nick pointed it out to the others, the animal charged and leapt at them in attack. The boys remembered what Mr. Thorpe had told them about not scattering. They picked up branches and sticks and fought for their lives. They managed to fight the wolf off, but all were cut and scratched and Jake had a nasty bite on his hand.

The boys headed back to camp, licking their wounds, so to speak, and discussing what to do. If they told their story, would anyone believe them? After the freak wolf attack on Mr. Thorpe the previous month, people would think that they were just making it up. In any case, a story that begins with "We'd just snuck out to pee our names in the snow…" isn't the kind of things that tends to build credibility! In the end they decided just to ice and bandage their wounds and slink off to bed.

The next morning Mr. Thorpe looked like he'd been in a fight. He made excuses about having gone for a leak in the night and tripped and fallen badly. The three boys looked a little tough too but they exchanged dark looks and kept their story to themselves. Who would believe them anyway?

Jake's mom, thank goodness, was not the kind to over-react to a little scratch, and it wasn't the first time Jake had come home from the woods with a minor puncture or six. She cleaned his bitten hand and accepted his story of having tripped and fallen into some piled buckthorn branches without much questioning.

All three boys got over their wounds quickly and the April campout was coming up fast. The other guys in Ben's patrol thought it was bit weird that he just insisted that they have venison tartar as part of the meal when they planned it, but Ben was a good guy, and that patrol will try anything once, so they figured, "What the heck?"

Mr. Thorpe was still running every day and looking even fitter than usual.

Two weeks after that March campout, David sidled up to Mr. Stern at troop meeting and asked, "Have you noticed that Mr. Thorpe seems to have a five o'clock shadow all over his head? It's like his hair has started to grow again."

Mr. Stern told David not to be so ridiculous "He should be so lucky!" was the parting shot.

The April campout was a week earlier than usual because of Spring Break. It went well. Spending more time around him, the boys saw that Mr. Thorpe really did seem to be growing back his hair. He almost had a crew-cut by the end of the weekend. On the boy side of things, Ben, Nick and Jake seemed to <u>really</u> dive into their food. The tartar was okay in most people's opinion — at least as okay as pureed raw meat with salt, pepper and a little chopped onion can ever be, but Ben seemed to just lap it up. Also, the burger Jake ate was practically mooing, but he obviously loved it. Nick's patrol had pre-cooked meatballs and you could tell that he was pretty disappointed. The food just didn't seem to be doing it for him on that trip.

The Tuesday after the camp Ben wasn't at troop meeting. Justin noticed that he didn't make it to school the following day either. Jake was feeling poorly too and stayed home, but nobody thought anything of it. Nick on the other hand was there, and just couldn't keep still. He kept scratching at the backs of his hands and he looked like he was wearing a wig. There was no way could he have grown that much hair in two days.

Mr. Thorpe was resplendent, however, with a head of hair that no-one thought could possibly be real. All the other adults were giving him grief about buying a toupé until he finally invited Alec, the SPL, up to give his hair a good tug to prove that it was real. Sure enough, if it was glued on, it wasn't coming off without a fight. With that full head of perfect black hair, the guy looked like some kind of Italian fashion model or movie star. It was really quite a transformation.

Ben was back at school by Friday, but he looked pale and had something of a haunted expression in his eyes. Harry and Jackson had noticed that Nick was out sick for the rest of the week, so Harry went over to Nick's house that Saturday to see if he was okay. He was met at the door by Nick's brother Patrick, who said that Nick's dad had taken him to the doctor. Then he said, "Check this out," and he took Harry to Nick's room.

The place was just trashed. It was as if a wild animal had gone berserk in there. Nick's entire collection of Beanie Babies had had their heads bitten off – even the little pink hippo he loved so much. Plus, every one of Nick's Miley Cyrus posters was slashed, as if by the claws of some rampaging wild animal.

Patrick wouldn't say what had happened, but it was pretty clear that it had scared the living daylights out of him.

Similar stories could have been told at Ben's and Jake's homes. Word spread around the boys' schools and all sort of jokes were soon being made. But each of the boys attended a different school, so nobody made a connection. Nobody, that is, except a kid named Sam.

Sam was a scout in the troop and a classmate of Jake's. One of Sam's grandfathers had come from Slovakia – a land of forests and mountains in eastern Europe. It happened that Sam's family went to visit him one weekend in early May, and he told his grandpa how people were joking that some of the boys in his troop had gone wild and torn up their rooms in the night. Sam expected his grandpa to laugh like everyone else did when he told the story. Instead Sam's grandpa got very serious, and asked him to tell all the details behind the story. So Sam told the story much as I have told it to you this evening. At this, Sam's grandpa told him to stay where he was and wait while he fetched something.

Grandpa came back with a wooden box the size of a shoe box. "There are things in the forest that man should fear," he said. "But there are ancient ways of protecting yourself. What weekend will you camp next?"

Sam answered and the old man said, "That's the next full moon. Open the box." The box contained a compact little Russian pistol and ten bullets with bright shiny tips. "Those are silver bullets. Take this with you on your next camping trip, just in case."

Sam protested that he shouldn't. The extent of the trouble he could get into for having a gun either at home or at scouts didn't bear thinking about, but his grandpa insisted so he took the gun with him that day. Two weeks later, full of worry as to what would happen if his dad or one of the other adults caught him with it, he packed the pistol up in his backpack for the troop outing that fell on the second weekend of May.

The troop went to the Woodman Center, where it's not uncommon to hear coyotes in the night. What was uncommon was that Nick, Ben and Jake decided to sleep together in the same tent. That wasn't a group of scouts you'd usually find bunking together.

It was cloudy during campfire that evening, but began to clear up towards ten o'clock when those three said that they were "tired out" for the day and, exchanging meaningful glances, slipped off to their tent. Mr. Thorpe too, seemed to be tired and out of sorts, and often looked up at the sky. He asked Mr. Stern and Mr. Hall to see to the end of the evening rituals, and went off to his bed a little early as well.

Sam was woken by barking and a long howl. He grabbed at his watch, pressed the light button and saw that it was 12:30. The barking started again, definitely moving closer. That pack of coyotes had to be planning to pass pretty close to the camp. When the howling started again, however, Sam decided that he needed to check it out. He dragged on his clothes, shook his tent-mate, Tanner, awake, and dug in his pack, pulling out the old Russian automatic. Sam pressed the clip home, checked that the safety was on, and stuffed the barrel into the waistband of his jeans before zipping up his jacket to cover it. You definitely want the safety on when it's in there, he thought. There's too much to lose if it goes off!

Sam and Tanner crawled out of their tent to see what they could see. The flap of one tent was wide open, and a quick look with a flashlight showed it to be empty. The clothes were all tossed to one side, obviously taken off in a hurry. It was the tent Ben, Nick and Jake were sharing.

The barking came again, closer now, with clear panting too. Whatever it was must be close. Sam and Tanner checked the wind – yes, the sounds and the wind were from the same direction. They were down-wind so the coyotes wouldn't smell them.

Suddenly, with no sound at all, a huge black dog – it had to be a German shepherd or a wolf – crashed through the side of a tent to their left. There was a vicious snarl followed by a scream that was sharply cut off.

"That was Mr. Stern's tent," Tanner whispered to Sam. The sounds coming from the tent were pretty clear. The animal was eating Mr. Stern. As Sam tried to figure out what to do, a commotion on the other side of him started as three smaller coyotes (or were they wolves too?) slashed their way into Alan and Justin's tent. These three didn't all look the same. Two of them seemed to be really light, almost blonde, in color, while the third was a much darker shade of brown. This attack, too, set off yells and screams of fear that quickly fell silent.

Sam was paralyzed with fear for a couple of seconds. Could this really be happening? "A scout is brave," Sam told himself, so he drew his pistol, chambered a round and walked over to Mr. Stern's tent. Tanner shone his light into the open gash, and there stood the wolf. It turned and gazed at the boys with hungry, malevolent eyes. Sam aimed, pulled the trigger and…

Nothing happened.

"The safety catch!" squeaked Tanner. "Take off the safety catch!"

The wolf looked a little puzzled and took one step towards them. "Now Sam, shoot it!" yelled Tanner. Sam reached around the gun, flipped off the safety catch, aimed at the still static wolf and **BANG!** fired right at its chest.

The animal dropped where it had stood and didn't move.

The noise, of both the attacks and the shot, was enough to wake the rest of the camp. The other boys were now coming out of their tents to see what was going on. Alec, Anthony and Eddie were hugging each other and crying with fright like a bunch of little girls. Matt was swearing up and down and begging *someone* to tell him what was going on, because he couldn't find his contact lens. Andrew and Jackson were staring in horrified fascination at the three tails sticking out of Alan and Justin's tent, and looking sick at the sounds coming from inside it. David was, of course, still fast asleep.

The three wolves that were eating Alan and Justin pulled out of the tent at the sound of the shot. They turned a cold gaze on Sam and Tanner and began to pace slowly toward them.

Sam didn't need too much time to figure out what to do. He aimed one quick shot at each wolf. Only the dark wolf turned and limped off, so he fired a second shot at the two that hadn't retreated yet. The dark-furred wolf was hobbling away on three legs, but Sam ran after it and shot it in the back, then he went back to the two blonde ones inside the camp and methodically shot each of them through the heart. Lastly he walked back over to the first and largest wolf, the one that had killed and eaten Mr. Stern. It was lying on its side and breathing heavily, bloody spittle dripping from its mouth. It watched Sam with its yellow eyes, not moving, knowing what was coming. "I'm sorry, Mr. Thorpe," Sam said, "but it's the only way."

The wolf closed its eyes, and Sam fired once into its chest. The gun's chamber hung open and the wolf's breathing stopped.

About this time, Matt found his contact lens, the older boys rediscovered their manhood, and David finally woke up.

Flashlights were found and the camp was searched. Jackson and Andrew swore that they saw the transformations back, but nobody besides them could be sure. There on the ground, dead as a couple of stones and naked as the day they were born, lay Jake and Ben. Outside the camp, shot in the butt and the back, lay Nick's corpse, and over on the edge of Mr. Stern's tent flap lay Mr. Thorpe. His face wore a quiet expression, and his head, which so recently had sported a mop of black hair, was completely bald.

The precise events that followed are not really worth recounting. Suffice it to say that Sam was not prosecuted for the shootings. A new scoutmaster was appointed, and Alan and Justin were mourned, but not for very long. Mr. Stern, of course, was irreplaceable, but the boys did decide that they needed a cool, young assistant scoutmaster around to help the SM and entertain all of them. They accomplished this by having Ross and Lawrence hack into the university registrar's computer and change all Zack's grades to C- or D. Sure enough, Zack was kicked out of college and returned home to live in his parents' basement. He now works at the local hardware store, and never misses a troop meeting or outing.

Troop 268 still exists today, and they still go on an outing every month, but they never, <u>ever</u> go star-gazing under a full moon.

4   The Curse of the Indian Mound

Author's Note

Camp Indian Mound is located outside Oconomowoc, WI and is owned by the Milwaukee County Council, Boy Scouts of America. I have no idea how it came to be a Boy Scout camp property. The story that follows is pure fiction and should in no way take away from the efforts and generosity of those who were actually behind the development of this wonderful camp.

In modern America we place headstones on the graves of those we bury to mark the spot so that others know who rests there. We view vandalism or desecration of a graveyard as a crime that is hard to understand and impossible to forgive.

Ancient peoples felt the same way about the places where they laid their mothers and fathers to rest. They too would place totems or curse markers on these burial places so that others might know them and treat them with the proper respect. Of course, these people lived in a world where the spirits of their ancestors were very real and did not necessarily pass forever into the happy hunting grounds. Violation of a curse marker could bring these spirits back to protect their resting places, and that is why, even tens or hundreds of years after the early residents of this state were forced off their traditional lands by the colonists, we must treat their burial places with respect and, perhaps, a little fear.

It was long the habit of the Winnebago peoples of the lands between Michi-gami and Kitchi-gummi (their names for the lakes we know as Lake Michigan and Lake Superior) to build mounds in the shapes of real or mythical creatures and to bury their dead in these mounds. Many fields of such mounds can be found, even today, all across the lands we call Wisconsin and along both sides of the St. Croix and Mississippi rivers. Some of these burial mounds are clearly marked. Others are lost to history, forgotten in woodlands, the curse markers rotted away over the years. Overgrown with brush or trees, these burial mounds, and their inhabitants, lie quietly. The spirits of their dead rest peacefully, unaware of the passage of time.

But you asked me to tell you a story, not give you a history lesson. The events I shall recount took place in 1975, and in most circles they would have been forgotten. Tonight, however, I will tell them to you and, perhaps someday, you will tell them to the next generation.

My story begins with a gift. It was in the fall of 1974 that the Dexter family gifted a summer cottage and 135 acres of woodland on the south shore of Silver Lake to their local Boy Scout Council. Such a gift comes along only rarely, and the scouts were keen to begin clearing parts of the land for what would become their best camping property ever. As soon as the ground was dry enough after the winter thaw, gangs of Arrowmen began travelling the twenty miles from the city to the camp each weekend. First they hiked the rolling ground, conducting a close survey and cutting trails with machetes and chainsaws as they did. Next, the Council camps committee laid out a plan of campgrounds, trails, a parade ground, latrines, a site for a dock for boating, a beach for swimming and a remodeling schedule to convert the small house by the roadside into an office and camp ranger's cabin.

The Arrowmen camped in a field by the lake-side and worked fast and with enthusiasm. Each weekend from May through the end of June, the landscape changed as trees were felled to make campsite clearings. Logs were cut and stacked or run through a saw to make boards. Holes were dug, posts placed and signs painted. The final touches were completed on Independence Day and on Saturday, July 7th, 1975, Camp Dexter opened for camping for Boy Scout troops.

Naturally, the many Arrowmen who had worked so hard on the camp were eager to show off their beautiful new camp to the younger scouts in their troops. Four times more scouts wanted to camp that weekend than the camp could hold, and the Council was forced to draw troop numbers from a hat to determine who got to go first. One of the lucky ones was Troop 6 from the Clark Square area. They would camp for three nights, Friday through Monday. It was the school holidays after all, and their SM was a teacher, so nobody had to work on Monday. The SPL, ASPL, troop guide and both patrol leaders had all participated in three weekends of work, and they had concentrated their efforts on a campsite named "Joliet" in honor of one of the early European explorers of the region. There were no camp roads so the boys and their leaders were obliged to pack everything the half mile from the parking area to Joliet camp. This went more or less as you would imagine. The younger boys whined about how heavy their packs were and how far they had to walk. The PLs shouldered most of the weight, including the patrol boxes. The troop guide brought up the rear, muttering encouragement to any of the younger guys who were lagging behind, and the "nature nerd" ASM insisted on identifying every tree and plant, especially the edible ones, as they passed it.

On reaching Joliet camp, the new boys and leaders found an area of dips and rises on a low bluff overlooking Silver Lake. Entirely sheltered from the wind on three sides, and with a few trees between the clearing and the drop to the lake, it truly was the perfect campsite.

The troop gear was unloaded and set up quickly. Next, of course, came personal tents. The weather forecast for the weekend included a possibility of thunderstorms, so everyone was careful to pitch their tents on one of the several low mounds that scattered the campsite. Everyone complimented the Arrowmen on the great job they had done of selecting such a fine site for the camp as the tent pegs slid easily into the soft earth. With the basics of the camp set up, everyone was hungry so duties were assigned and a roster for the weekend posted. The ASPL, with some grumbling, took three scouts with shovels off behind a mound on the west side of camp to dig a latrine trench and put up a screen while the rest set about the serious business of cooking dinner.

The latrine crew was surprised to find a variety of bits of pottery and even a couple of arrow-heads in the dirt as they dug. It was a regular treasure trove for young boys, but nothing terribly unusual in those days. After dinner, they built up a fire, practiced a couple of skits for summer camp that was coming up at the end of the month, then settled into telling jokes and stories as the light faded. At ten-thirty the Scoutmaster called for lights out and when, fifteen minutes later, the bugler croaked his way through taps, half the troop was already too sound asleep to hear it.

Now all of this may sound very idyllic and ordinary. So it was, until about three in the morning when a couple of the older boys awoke to find that the temperature in their tent had dropped uncomfortably. It had been warm when they went to bed, and they were lying on top of their sleeping bags, so they climbed into their sacks and tried to fall asleep again. It wasn't easy, however. For a long time they couldn't quite put their finger on what was keeping them up. Talking it over as the light of dawn started to penetrate the tent, they decided that it was two things. One was a feeling of not being entirely alone. The other had to be, they decided, a mole, that insisted on scurrying back and forth through a very shallow tunnel under their tent. There was no other explanation for it. Something was definitely moving about in the dirt under the tent floor. Eventually they did drop back off into a fitful sleep, but imagine their surprise the next day when the occupants of five out of the eight tents reported the same experience. Who knew there could be so many moles in one area? And they hadn't hit a single tunnel when they'd dug the latrine?

Saturday was terrific. The temperature rose fast that July day, and by ten the boys were almost all in the lake swimming, diving for freshwater mussels, or paddling about in the inflatable dinghy the scoutmaster had brought along for the fun of it. At one o'clock, the scoutmaster called them all back to camp to get "dry on the outside and wet on the inside" as he liked to say – insisting that every kid drink at least one quart of water for every 80 pounds of body weight. He was a math teacher – if something could be done by a formula, it was. They ate too, of course. The heat of the day was spent in the shade. Some kids read books, some whittled sticks, others worked on scoutcraft with the troop guide. One patrol leader even got some boys together and turned several hundred feet of baler twine into a hammock for the SPL. That was a pretty cool project that earned the scouts who did it an exemption from washing up duty for the whole weekend.

To work up an appetite for dinner, they finished the day with a pioneering project. There were more downed tree limbs than you could count still lying in camp from all of the tree clearing that had been done. Two hours of sawing, climbing, lashing and tying later, a ten foot by eight foot platform stood high in a swamp oak tree by the lakeside. It had posts and a railing around it, and twine zig-zagging all around between the railing and deck so that nobody would roll out during the inevitable goofing around that would occur up there. By the time the tree-house was complete everyone needed another swim to get the sweat and grime off themselves, so dinner was late and the light was failing by the time they sat down around the campfire to reflect on the day. There were fewer stories told that night, and heads nodded as many scouts fought to stay awake as they stared into the flames. Half the troop had already gone to bed when the scoutmaster called for taps. The bugler was one of those, so it was a quiet end to the day.

That night, the same sort of thing happened in the same five tents. Again the boys awoke in the small hours of the morning to find their tents unnaturally cold. Again they felt *something* moving about under the floors of their tents. The next day, one of them would describe it as being like somebody running a stick back and forth under the plastic; back and forth, as if trying to get through. But this night, there was not only the feeling of an additional presence in the tent, there was also a sound - the sound of a faint chanting and drumming, as if coming from very far away – perhaps from the other side of the lake. "What kind of an idiot plays music on a lake-side at two in the morning?" the SPL wondered out loud that Sunday morning.

There were ten pairs of sandy eyes and some pretty grumpy faces when the scouts rolled out of bed. The boys whose sleep had been interrupted were not in a good humor, and a thundershower that came through, interrupting breakfast, extinguishing their fire, and soaking everything, did nothing to improve their tempers. The scouts sat under a rain-fly watching the ground steam as it dried in the sunshine that followed the storm front. Bored, many of them poked at the ground with sticks, digging little holes and looking at what they found. To their surprise, even this level of digging uncovered some more Indian artifacts. One more arrow-head, what the ASM thought was a stone axe-head, and even some beads carved out of bone were pulled out of the shallow holes, cleaned off and lined up on a small tarp for inspection. The thought of this wonderful haul of souvenirs brightened the general mood and the SM finished the cheering-up process by pulling a bag of butterscotch candies out of his tent. "Whatever happened to 'no edibles in tents', Mr. Schmidt?" asked the SPL with a sly grin. "The bag was sealed, and I figure the smell of my boots is strong enough to cover anything a 'coon could pick up from the outside of the bag," came the reply. That got a good laugh all around.

They sent runners to some of the other camps to see what was happening about Sunday services. Everyone was running late because of the rain, and by general agreement, everyone in camp went to the parade ground at eleven-thirty for a Scouts' Own Service. Every other troop in camp left that afternoon, and by two o'clock, as the heat and humidity rose, Troop 6 had Camp Dexter to themselves. The lake, of course, beckoned. A rope swing was constructed on a tree-limb at the water's edge and the afternoon was spent swinging, splashing, swimming, and finally agonizing over sunburn as the entire troop, adults included, sat around, shirtless and gently glowing, in the shade of the swamp oaks around the camp.

Dinner was Scout Stew prepared in one of two enormous pots. The other contained five pounds of random pasta – a mixture of five different one pound bags of pasta in various colors and shapes. They ate it in the tree-house. Everyone was tired and sunburned, and looking forward to going home the next day. Several of the boys joked that it wouldn't matter how cold things got in their tents tonight. They were all glowing like electric heaters to keep it warm. There was no moon that night, and the stars were clear as they sat around the campfire. One first class scout was into astronomy, and he went out by the lake with a small group of boys who all lay on their backs picking out constellations. Before lights-out, the SM got up and told a story - an Indian legend about how the Great Spirit had placed the stars in the sky and drawn out the shapes of the animals in the heavens.

Another storm front moved in at four o'clock that Monday morning. Four scouts and two leaders were awoken by the crash of thunder, flash of lighting and the hiss of rain running down the walls of their rain-flies. After half an hour of steady rain, Mr. Schmidt decided he'd better go and see if the scouts were staying dry. They were all on higher ground, so they should be alright.

All the tents were standing and none was surrounded by water, though there was some standing water in the gullies between the mounds where the tents were pitched. He went to the SPL's tent and shook it a little to see if the boys were awake. Getting no response, he unzipped the door and reached inside to shake the boy awake and get him to go around and check in with his scouts. Imagine his surprise when he saw his breath condense in front of him and felt the chill in the tent. There was actually frost on the inside walls of the tent. How in the world could that be? A little panicked, he slapped his hand down on a sleeping bag and found it empty. Grabbing the sack out into the open, he realized that it was cut open along the bottom - a ragged gash with feathers pouring out of either side. Under the bag, the mat and floor of the tent were similarly ripped, and there was no trace of the boys.

The two leaders checked the rest of the tents and found four others in the same state. They took their remaining four scouts to the parking lot, and since no permanent ranger had been assigned to the camp, they drove to a gas station to phone the Scout Executive's emergency number and the County Sheriff. Leaving the boys at the gas station with change to call their parents on the pay-phone, Mr. Schmidt and his assistant drove back to Camp Dexter and jogged back to Joliet camp to begin investigating. They moved one of the tents and found the ground under it completely undisturbed. Whatever had ripped through the tents had not touched the ground. But could ten boys really have ripped through their sleeping bags, bed-rolls and tent floors from *inside* their bags? Within an hour a full blown search of Camp Dexter was under way. The ten missing scouts' parents, friends and neighbors joined the police in a close search of every nook and cranny in the 135-acre reservation. Police divers examined the bottom of Silver Lake but nobody found a thing. It wasn't until two o'clock in the afternoon that anybody thought of the tree-house. Could there be ten boys watching from up there, giggling away as all these adults searched franticly for them? No. The tree-house too was empty.

The following morning the decision was made to dig down into the earth below where the tents had stood. Shall I tell you what they found? Are you sure you want to know?

Four feet beneath each tent they found the bodies of the scouts. Still in their pajamas, the scouts were all dead. A look of sheer horror on his face, his mouth filled with earth and fixed in a silent scream, each scout was caught in the cold embrace of the skeleton of a long dead Indian.

An aerial survey of the Dexter property showed it to be littered with Indian mounds. Archeologists labeled it as one of the most extensive such sites in eastern Wisconsin. It did, however, present the Milwaukee Scout Council with a bit of problem. What do you with a campground where your scouts get killed by the spirits of long dead Indians? The solution, they decided, was to make it into a cub camp. They would abandon Joliet camp, renaming it "Winnebago point". They created new camp sites in level areas and put up several buildings for scouts to sleep in, checking carefully to make sure that they did not build over any burial mounds. Each building would have a poured, steel reinforced concrete floor – just in case. The buildings were named for the youth leaders among the scouts who died that July night: Teerlink, Harnischfeger, Stowe and Christl. Camp Dexter itself was renamed *Camp Indian Mound*, and all who come there now are taught to respect the mounds that are clearly marked in the camp. Many more buildings and facilities have been constructed at Camp Indian Mound over the years, and the names of the young scouts who died have been lost to history, but those who know the story of the Curse of the Indian Mound still have trouble sleeping when the temperature drops sharply at night, when something moves under their tent floor, or when the sound of drums drifts across the lake.

5 The Creature in the Ravine

If you have talked with scouts or camp counselors from the southern part of the Glacier's Edge Council, you may have learned of a strange legend. Apparently there is a creature that haunts the ravine behind Allen Hall at Camp Indian Trails (CIT). A faceless, deathly pale creature is said to appear to scouts who venture into the ravine, and sometimes to those who cross the bridge alone.

Scouts seem to love scary stories, and the boys who come to CIT to camp lap up these tales. They even tell them to the younger scouts to scare them when they camp near the ravine at CIT, or when they trek though it on their way back to their campsite after campfires.

Now, it happened that one January Troop 628 was staying in Allen Hall. They had also reserved Chemokemon Lodge, which stands on the other side of the ravine. The lodge was to be home to the new scout patrol, called the Roadrunners, for the weekend. They, the ASPL and a couple of Star Scout troop guides were to stay there together and work on finishing skills and crafts needed for first class rank so that all of them could pass into regular patrols after the upcoming court of honor. The rest of the troop was to camp in the basement of Allen Hall.

All the cooking and eating was to be done in the kitchen and dining hall at Allen Hall, and so it was that after getting moved in on Friday evening, everyone gathered in the dining area at Allen Hall for cracker barrel. The patrol leader of the Roadrunners, Justin, decided to head back to the lodge a little before the rest of his patrol. He wanted a few minutes to think his way through the next day's activities and responsibilities, post his patrol duty roster and generally make sure that he had a plan and knew how to work it.

The ground was icy, and Justin was looking down at his feet as he walked to make sure that he didn't slip. His thoughts were on the following morning's plan, and actually looking where he was going was not really occupying much of his attention.

That's why he practically walked into it. He was half way across the bridge when some sixth sense told him to look up. There, in the beam of his flashlight, was a deathly pale creature the size of a small man. Its face was unrecognizable. It wore tattered clothing that covered most of its body, and on being lit by Justin's light, it turned and bolted back across the bridge the way it had come.

A scout is brave, and Justin was no exception, but in this case, he was also surprised enough to drop his flashlight, which bounced over the edge of the bridge into the ravine. He was also very aware of the fact that he was alone, which is never good, so he turned around and high-tailed it back to Allen Hall as fast as his legs could carry him. He went straight to the SPL and told him what he'd seen. The SPL laughed and said that it was a nice try for Justin to wind up his fellow first years, but they really did need to get back to the lodge and bed. Besides, winding the young guys up was the older guys' job; calming them down was Justin's. Justin didn't argue. If he were in the SPL's shoes, he wouldn't take him seriously either.

Justin and the ASPL led the Roadrunners back over the bridge to Chemokemon Lodge and started settling in for the night. The ASPL told them all to quiet down and get into their bunks, and was just about to climb into his own bunk when he suddenly screamed and dropped his teddy bear on the floor.

"What's the matter?" somebody yelled.

"There, at the window … a pale white face! It was horrible!" the ASPL stammered.

"Aw, come on!" said one of the Roadrunners. "You're just trying to scare us. The SPL said it was the older scouts' job. We're not *that* easy to pick on, you know."

"No. Really, it was right there at the window by my bed!" said the ASPL, pointing at the window next to his bunk.

"Yeah, right. Pull the other one," replied another first year. "Come on guys, let's get to bed!"

The ASPL picked up his bear and grumbled that nobody ever took him seriously. He climbed into his bunk, hunched up on one elbow with a copy of Boy's Life magazine, and said, "Ten minutes to lights-out!"

It was about five minutes after this that a kid named Spencer screamed and pointed at a window on the opposite side of the lodge from the ASPL's bunk. "It's there! I saw it too!" he exclaimed.

"Give it up already!" shouted one of the other guys. Somebody whacked Spencer over the back of the head with a pillow, which inevitably started a cabin-wide pillow fight. It took a good three or four minutes for the ASPL and the patrol guides to restore order, though it must be said that all three of them managed to land a few good strikes before they actually attempted to stop the conflict. After that, everyone was tired enough that the whole cabin was silent save for gentle snoring by 10:45.

The next morning, the scouts looked outside the windows where the alleged monster appearances had occurred and found footprints in the snow. The left foot was a sneaker print with a tear in the sole. The right was a boot, two sizes larger than the left.

They followed the footprints away from the lodge, through the snow and down into the ravine. There, the prints became lost amid the undergrowth and a mess of other prints made by scouts from another troop who had come through on snowshoes the day before. There wasn't time for an extensive search; pancakes and bacon were on the menu for breakfast, and bacon trumps everything in Troop 628.

Saturday went much as Saturdays do. The first years worked with the ASPL and the troop guides, completing requirements for first class, practicing all their knots, working on signaling, and making codes for each other to break. The older guys split up and worked on a couple of merit badges. Then they followed the SM all over the camp on snow shoes and met up with the first years for lunch. This was followed by an almighty snowball fight with another troop and a camp-wide quinzee building competition in the afternoon. Troop 628's quinzee was, of course, the winner for sheer size. When you have 25 boys to shovel the snow you can build a *really* big quinzee.

Daylight starts to fade at about 4:30 in the Rock River valley in January and it was also about that time that thick, fluffy snowflakes began to fall. The scouts took this as their cue to go inside and start the task of cooking dinner. There's a large kitchen at Allen Hall, so there were a lot of boys involved in the cooking, with the other half of the troop playing board or card games out in the main dining hall or down in the bunk room in the basement. After dinner they had a campfire program in front of the fireplace in the dining room. The fire gave the only heat in that part of the building, so it was a chilly affair and they didn't drag it out.

After hot chocolate and cookies for cracker barrel, Justin led his patrol back across the bridge with the ASPL at his side, shining his flashlight through the snow, which was falling harder now. Halfway across they practically bumped into a figure as pale as the snow itself. This time the creature loosed a paleolithic bellow before turning and fleeing across the bridge. The creature veered to the left and jumped into the ravine at the end of the bridge. It ran down the slope towards the stream-bed and at the same time angled right, through Pioneer campsite, and towards the dense woodland that lies between Allen Hall and Clark Lodge, up by the main road. The scouts gave chase. Justin stopped two of his Roadrunners and sent them back to Allen Hall to tell the rest of the troop what was happening. Then, he dashed off through the snow after the others, following the clear footprints in the fresh snow. Falling snow muffled the sounds as the scouts charged through the night, chasing down the creature that had so surprised them.

When Justin caught up to his patrol, he was surprised to find them standing looking at two sets of fresh footprints going in two different directions. Which way did the creature go? They were so close behind it, how could it have managed to leave two sets of tracks? Did it have a mate with whom it was now setting an ambush for them?

The Roadrunners divided into two groups. Justin took two boys after one set of footprints while Luke and the ASPL took two others, following the second set of tracks. They called back and forth for a little while, but the snow masked their voices as well as their vision, and they soon lost track each other's location.

It didn't take long for both groups to become completely disoriented in the thick brush and heavily falling snow. Moving quietly now, with flashlights off to avoid showing their position, Justin's group crept forward, listening for any sound of movement or the heavy breathing of a monster on the run. Justin stepped around a large tree and was confronted with the snow-blurred outline of a man-like shape, standing on a fallen tree, towering above him. The creature leapt onto Justin, pushing him back into the other two scouts in his search party. Justin felt multiple hands pin him to the ground and snow was swept into his face. The shock of the attack and the cold made it hard for him to fight back. A flashlight lit up in front of his face and a gloved hand wiped across it, getting the snow out of his eyes.

"Oh. It's just you!?" said a voice he knew.

"Get off him guys. It's Justin." It was Luke's voice. "The monster must've run a circle and made us bump into each other."

Luke's party helped Justin and his two buddies to their feet and dusted the snow off them. They turned their flashlights on and followed the tracks all the way around the circle they described. Nowhere could they see where the creature might have left the trail after completing the circle. Besides, some of them had big feet, and they had now left so many tracks of their own that with the falling snow blurring the outline of each footprint it was impossible to tell the creature's tracks from their own.

As the Roadrunners searched, they heard other voices coming up the valley. The Scoutmaster and half a dozen of the older boys came up through the snow with mischievous grins on their faces. "Catch anything?" the Scoutmaster asked.

"Only Justin," Luke replied. "Whatever the creature is, it's pretty smart. It left us a false trail and when we split up we just ended up jumping each other."

"I think that's enough excitement for tonight. It's past lights-out, and you guys are so wound up that it'll take another hour for you get to sleep if you're lucky. Back to the cabin, all of you."

It had been a pretty good monster chase, they all agreed, but only Justin and the ASPL had actually seen the creature. They talked as they headed back to Chemokemon Lodge, making sure that they agreed on what the thing had looked like. The Scoutmaster was right. It did take them a long time to get to sleep that night. Two of the 8th graders popping up at the cabin windows and shining flashlights on their faces about ten minutes after they turned the lights out *definitely* didn't help matters!

In the morning, all of CIT was covered in a seven-inch blanket of snow. Justin, Luke, Pete and Spencer grabbed snow shoes from the trailer and went back down into the ravine after breakfast to see what they could find, but all that was left of last night's chase were gentle depressions in the snow where their footprints had been. As they hiked back up to Allen Hall from the floor of the ravine, they heard snow fall from a branch somewhere farther up the valley. Looking back to where they had searched the previous night, they saw brush moving. It was moving as brush will move when something large pushes its way through it.

There were only four of them, however. Four young scouts against something smart enough to lead them in circles in the night and big enough to move the brush as it moved through it. The SPL was calling for all the scouts to gather up their gear and pack the trailer so that they could leave. There clearly wasn't time to go back up there and look for whatever that thing was.

So the Roadrunners rejoined their troop, stowed the snowshoes in the trailer, went back to the Lodge to make sure that their patrol hadn't left any gear, and then climbed into a van for the drive home. Whatever the white-faced creature in the ravine was, it would still be there for them to search for next time they came.

And so it would. And so it is to this day; watching, waiting. Sometimes it dares to come up close to Allen Hall, or even to walk out onto the bridge. Who will be the next scout, I wonder, to bump into *The Creature in the Ravine*?

6 The Fog on the Lake

The story begins with a troop of Wisconsin scouts who had decided to camp by Devil's Lake for the weekend. This was high impact camping at its finest, and they rolled into the group camp with minivans, pick-up trucks, and a twelve-foot trailer stuffed with tents, bags of gear, E-Z ups, screen-tents, Dutch ovens, stoves.....everything you need to have a weekend in the woods and eat really well. The sun was setting below the West Bluff, casting the valley into shadow, but leaving the sky bright and lighting up the crest of the East Bluff in a fiery orange on the red of the quartzite rock and the green of the trees as it sank down to mark the end of the day. The temperature was already beginning to drop as the boys pitched their tents, set up their kitchen areas and assembled the E-Z ups to cover the kitchen areas in an effort to keep everything from being soaked by the dew.

Once camp was set up, the SPL told the patrol leaders to take their boys exploring. Maps of the park were handed out and the PLs tuned their radios to a common frequency, then set off with their patrols to find the important things in the park. I refer of course to the latrines, the swimming beach, the concession stand and the soda machine. A thin fog was already beginning to form over the lake as the first patrols got to the shore. It thickened as the boys skimmed stones and picked their way among the rocks at the lake-side in the fading light. The pale blue of the daytime sky faded into midnight blue with a promise of inky black and the first stars began to shine. By the time the boys of the Cobra patrol set off back to camp, the fog had thickened to the point that you couldn't even see the water unless you were right next to it. The fog continued to rise slowly up over the rocks at the water's edge.

The Cobra patrol was a young bunch. Their APL, Dale, was barely thirteen, and the rest of the gang were a mixture of first and second year scouts ranging from "not quite eleven yet" to twelve. Dale stopped the group for a last look at the fog covered lake before they headed across the field by the swim beach to walk back to the campground, and that was when they saw it. The fog in the middle of the lake seemed to swirl briefly, then a mound formed, and moved across the lake towards the shore where they had recently been standing. It was like looking at a mole track forming across the fog, except that it settled back down behind the mole. The fog surface became level again as the unseen object reached the shore, and all was still. "What *was* that?" one of the first years asked Dale. Dale was under clear instructions NOT to go scaring the first years on what was, in many cases, their first campout with the troop, so he squashed his instinct to suggest something creepy or dangerous and said, "Probably just a duck that fell asleep before the fog formed and woke up with a strong need for dry ground." He added a little chuckle at his own joke, just for effect, and watched as the first years breathed a collective sigh of relief. Still, he wondered. What *was* that?! Casting a glance back over his shoulder as they reached the trail into the woods that would lead them back to their campsite in the south campground, Dale noticed that the fog was spilling over the edge of the lake and up onto the grass. "<u>That</u> is pretty darn spooky looking," he thought to himself.

The Cobras returned to the campground just in time for the evening's campfire. They ended at 9:30 and opened some cookies for cracker-barrel, then turned for their tents. Dale noticed that wisps of fog were beginning to appear between the trees and the air had taken on an odd chill. The sky above him was completely clear, and he took a few minutes to gaze at the Milky Way before crawling into his tent, shoving his tent-mate off his sleeping pad and kicking off his boots before slipping into his sleeping bag. "Who needs to brush teeth or put on pajamas anyway?" he thought. "One night isn't going to kill me."

Dale was woken up by loud squawking from a nearby turkey vulture nest shortly before three a.m. Unable to get back to sleep, he decided to get up and stretch his legs a little. When he quietly unzipped his tent flap, the camp was lit by pale light from a three-quarter moon, and he was surprised to find that there was a little over a foot of fog covering the ground between the tents. He played with it for a moment, tracing patterns in it with his finger before crawling out of his tent and congratulating himself on his wisdom in not taking off his clothes. He pulled on his boots, stood up, and cast his glance around the camp. All was quiet and motionless, except for a slight wave action in the layer of fog. Over by the fire pit, however, a small figure stood alone and motionless, its hands out over the fire pit, apparently trying to extract some warmth from the long ago extinguished fire. The figure by the fire was of a size that could only be a first year, which meant that it was probably one of Dale's guys, so he trudged over to see why the kid was up by himself in the middle of the night.

When he reached the fire ring and trained his flashlight on the figure, however, he was shocked to find not an eleven year old scout, but a small man in an impeccably cut black pin-striped suit. The guy looked like he'd just stepped out of a concert hall or a business meeting. His black hair was slicked down and he wore a closely trimmed moustache and goatee, also black, but with a hint of gray that gave him a distinguished appearance.

"Would you mind not pointing that light into my eyes young man?" the small man said. He had an odd accent, not Midwestern; perhaps Boston or New York? Dale couldn't be sure. He'd never made a point of learning that sort of thing.

"Excuse me," said Dale pointing his light down into the fog that came up to both their knees, "but I thought you were one of my scouts. This is a scout troop camp site for the weekend. I don't think you're supposed to be here."

The man smiled in the moonlight. "Dear boy," he said, "this entire park is mine and I may go where I please."

Dale didn't know quite what to say. The little man continued to smile and reached his hands back out over the fire pit. "Pity you put it out," he remarked to no one in particular. "I rather like the warmth of a good fire."

Finally, Dale recovered enough of his wits to say, "Sir, please leave our camp right now. This is a little weird, and I think I'll have to wake the scoutmaster if you don't go right away." Saying this, Dale began to walk slowly around the fire pit to place himself between it and the SM's tent.

"Calm down, dear boy. I mean no harm. It is a beautiful night and we two are both up and able to enjoy it. Let us rekindle the fire and talk a while." At this, he waved his hand at the fire pit and the coals instantly sprang back into life, emitting a warm red glow under small blue and yellow flames. The fog seemed to retreat from the fire ring a little, but never quite left the point where the little man stood. A few tendrils of it still connected his legs to the larger sea of mist that stood throughout the campsite.

"That's a neat trick," Dale said, stepping in closer to the fire and warming his hands over it. "How'd you do that?"

"That?" asked the little man. "Oh, that's a simple trick. I have a particular affinity for fire you see." He flashed a quick smile at Dale and offered a handshake. "My name's Cypher. Louis Cypher."

Dale again found himself at something of a loss. He was not by nature a rude boy, and refusing the man's handshake would certainly have been rude. The guy seemed pleasant enough, and he was so small that Dale didn't really see any threat in him. Good manners prevailed, and Dale stepped forward and shook his hand. It was a good, firm handshake, much to Dale's relief.

"Can you teach me how to do that trick with the fire?" Dale asked. "You'd be amazed at how handy that would be for a scout."

"Oh, I could teach you many tricks if you really choose to learn. I could offer you a number of favors, too - things that would make your life much easier." Cypher's smile was wide and genuine in the firelight. It was the kind of smile that simultaneously invites you in, and sends a shiver of warning up your spine.

Dale frowned and asked, "Why would you offer to teach me tricks and do favors for me? This is pretty odd, sir. I think you'd better explain yourself or leave our camp."

"My, my! You are a touchy fellow, aren't you?!" replied Cypher. "Allow me to explain then. I do not make such an offer lightly. What I offer you is a simple deal. I will do some things for you to make your life easier, and in return, I will ask that you do some simple things for me."

"What, like mow your lawn?" asked Dale.

"No, not that," replied Cypher. "Nothing so strenuous. You might even rather enjoy the things I'll ask you to do. Now why don't you tell me what sort of things you're struggling with and we'll see if I can help." At this, Mr. Cypher sat himself down in somebody's forgotten folding chair and placed his hands together in front of his chest, as if preparing for a negotiation.

Dale decided to run with this and see what was on offer. "Well.... could you get me out of kitchen clean-up duty for the weekend?" Dale asked.

"No trouble" replied the man. "Next?"

Dale was surprised, so he kept going. "How about getting all those darned knots and lashings to stick in my mind? It seems like anything tougher than a square knot just won't work for me."

"Trickier, but yes, I can do that for you. Next?" Cypher now had a legal pad in his hand and was scribbling notes.

Dale was starting to enjoy himself. "How about merit badges? Can you arrange for me to get all the Citizenship merit badges at the next Court of Honor?"

"Why stop there?" replied Cypher. "I could throw in Lifesaving, Personal Management and Family Life, AND make the troop records reflect five additional service hours. You'd earn Star Scout at that Court of Honor you mentioned."

"But wouldn't the scoutmaster and the Troop Committee know that I hadn't done the work?" asked Dale.

"I can fix it so that they think you did," came the reply.

This was starting to sound too good to be true. "How?" Dale asked, the doubt clear in his voice.

Cypher's voice had an edge to it as he replied, "All things are possible if you make a deal with me."

"How do I know you can do what you're offering?" Dale asked.

The small man shook his head and muttered, "People just don't seem to trust me. Do I look untrustworthy to you?"

Dale said "No." He didn't look untrustworthy; it was just that the things he was offering sounded a little far-fetched.

"Very well. I will give you your first request for free as proof of my good faith," said Cypher. He put down his notepad and reached down into the fog by his feet. When he stood up again, he had a six foot length of soft rope in his hand. He threw this to Dale. "Tie a bowline in the end of that," he commanded.

Dale considered for a moment and then went through the motions as if it was second nature. He muttered the instructions under his breath as he went. "Make a loop, right over left. The snake came out of the hole, went round the tree and back into the hole. Pull the head and the tail with one hand and the tree with the other and ... HEY! IT WORKED!" Dale was thrilled.

"Try something trickier. Sheep Shank!" commanded Cypher. Once again Dale found his mind commanding his hands and in seconds he had a nice, stable sheep shank tied between his hands.

"Cool man!" Dale exclaimed. Dropping the rope back at the small businessman's feet, he said, "You have yourself a deal!"

"Excellent!" said Cypher with a broad, satisfied smile. "Just sign here," and he handed the notepad to Dale. There were several pages of text in spidery handwriting and at the end of it a line with an X next to it. Dale scribbled his signature on the line. The text of the notes was black, but as Dale signed, the ink from the pen was red. It was clear to see, even in the silver moonlight that illuminated the camp.

"We have a deal young man," said Cypher. "I will do as I have promised, and you must do the same. Do not break faith with me. Those who have done so have never failed to regret it."

At this, the small man dropped the notepad into a leather briefcase that Dale hadn't noticed before, and walked briskly off in the direction of the lake. The fog swirled around his legs as he walked, and he seemed to shrink into it as he disappeared from the moonlight at the edge of the campsite. Dale felt cold all of a sudden. He turned back to the fire to warm his hands, but the fire was out. No warmth rose from it.

Shoving his cold hands into his pockets, Dale walked slowly back to his tent. He crawled inside, got back into his sleeping bag, and quickly fell into a troubled and dreamy sleep. He dreamt that he was in front of the troop receiving his Star Scout badge. When Dale woke up to the bugler's call the next morning, he wasn't sure if any of what he thought he remembered from the night was real. Maybe it was all a dream.

Dale went to check the duty roster for breakfast. Last he remembered, he'd been down for clean up, but looking at the roster, his name wasn't there. In fact, his name wasn't on the duty roster at all. Maybe Mr. Cypher had been real and good to his word? Dale snuck quietly back to his tent, pulled a comic book out of his day-pack and settled down on top of his sleeping bag to read.

An hour or so later, Dale's tent-mate came looking for him and announced that breakfast was ready. Dale stuck the comic in his back pocket while he ate, and simply hung around the picnic table reading after he was done. The other guys in his patrol took care of the dishes without complaint. One of the first years even grabbed Dale's mess kit, washed it, and hung the whole thing up to dry in its mesh bag when he was done. Nobody seemed to notice or care that Dale wasn't helping. This, Dale had to admit, was pretty cool.

After breakfast, as they were walking over to the West Bluff to begin a hike around the lake, the scoutmaster pulled up next to Dale. He wished him a good morning, then said, "Make sure you catch up with me for a scoutmaster's conference this weekend. The advancement coordinator tells me you've completed all your requirements for Star."

"Definitely cool," thought Dale.

The land at the south end of the West Bluff has always been swampy and this weekend was no exception. The troop walked across it on board-walks. The kid in front of Dale was a second year named Mark. Mark was not the only annoying kid in the troop, but he was certainly the one who most got under Dale's skin.

As they walked, Cypher's voice sounded as a whisper in Dale's mind. "Trip him," was what it said.

Dale stopped suddenly, and the kid behind almost walked into his back. "Get a move on, Dale," came the other boy's voice.

Cypher's voice sounded in his mind again, "I said, trip him. It's part of your end of our deal."

Dale got over his surprise and thought, "Well, it IS Mark, it WOULD be really funny, and what's the harm anyway?"

With that, he swung his leg and deftly hooked Mark's left foot behind his right. Mark went down sideways off the board-walk and landed on his face in soft, black mud. As he pulled himself up, the entire troop turned to look and began to laugh. He really was a sight, black from head to toe and ankle deep in mud. With a terrific squelch, he pulled his feet out of the mud and climbed back up onto the board-walk.

"Feeling clumsy?" Dale asked him with a grin. Mark just wiped mud out of his eyes, and turned back to his walking, saying nothing. "If that's all Cypher's going to ask of me, this is going to be the best deal I've ever made," Dale thought to himself.

They began climbing up the bluff. About half way up, the SPL called for a water break. Mark was still next to Dale, the mud beginning to dry on his skin and clothes. Mark's water bottle was the wide mouth kind, and as he tilted it back to drink, Cypher's voice sounded in Dale's head again. "Dump his water in his face."

This time Dale didn't even hesitate. He stood up with his pack in his hands and deliberately used it to knock the water bottle upwards out of Mark's grip. About half the water went into Mark's face and the rest went down his chest. "Kid, you really are feeling clumsy today," Dale laughed. Mark just looked at his empty water bottle with despair and pushed it back into his day-pack.

"Very good my boy," echoed Cypher's voice in Dale's mind.

At the top of the West Bluff there is a lookout that makes a great stopping point to catch your breath after the long climb. Here, the SPL said to drink again, and Mark just looked at his shoes and cast a longing look at Dale's water bottle as Dale took a long, cool drink. Once again, Dale found himself next to Mark as they stood taking in the awesome view over the lake and the frightening 300 foot drop to jagged rocks below.

Cypher's voice sounded in Dale's head again. "Push him off," it said.

Dale stood frozen. Could Cypher be serious? This was too much. If he pushed Mark off that ledge he would almost certainly die.

"I said push him off," came the voice again. "What are you waiting for? We have a deal."

"No!" Dale threw the thought back at the place in his mind where Cypher's voice seemed to come from.

"Do not break faith with me," replied Cypher's voice. "You have made your deal with the Devil. Now push him off!"

"No!" Dale shouted in his mind. Dale could feel a wave of anger wash over him from inside his mind. It made him feel dizzy. His balance was going. There was nothing he could do about it. The ledge seemed to be coming closer, but his legs were like Jello. Dale knew in that instant. He was falling over the edge.

They say that your life flashes before your eyes in the moment that you are about to die. All Dale saw was Cypher's face, staring into his. Instead of the falling sensation he expected, however, Dale saw Cypher's face suddenly change. It became younger, and muddier, and its mouth opened and said, "Dude, are you okay? I thought you were going to pitch right over the edge there! Do you get sick from heights?"

Mark strained to hold up Dale's mostly limp body in a bear hug. He pushed Dale back over his center of gravity, landing Dale on his butt with Mark lying on top of him. Mark climbed off Dale and asked again, "Are you okay?"

He dug into Dale's pack, pulled out Dale's water bottle and handed it to him. "Have a drink and you'll be fine. Come on!"

Dale took a drink from the bottle, then sat looking at it for a moment. He held the bottle out to Mark. "Thanks, Mark. Sorry I spilled your water back there." Mark just grinned, took a short drink, and handed the bottle back.

The rest of the hike was uneventful. The mud on Mark's face and clothes dried out and flaked off for the most part. Dale walked quietly and kept his head down as he hiked. No voice whispered in Dale's mind. One thing did keep coming back into Dale's thoughts, however. Cypher's voice had said, "You have made your deal with the Devil."

Could it really be? What was it Cypher had said last night? "This entire park is mine." And his name - Louis Cypher. There was something a little too familiar in that. Louis Cypher, Louey Cypher, Lou….. Lou Cypher – Lucifer!

"You made a deal with the Devil, alright," Dale thought to himself. What's going to happen now?

Dale stayed well back from the cliff edge for the rest of the hike. He picked his way down the steep parts using his hands for extra balance. Getting back to the camp, he headed straight for his tent, tripped over a stump hidden by some long grass and sprawled flat on his face. As he picked himself up he couldn't help thinking that he heard a familiar voice chuckling in the dark places of his mind.

Dale had barely twenty minutes of rest before his PL came over and said, "Get moving, Dale. You're cooking tonight!"

"What?" Dale asked. "I wasn't on the roster for dinner this morning." "Well you are now, buddy. Move it!" came the reply. Dale walked over the duty roster and stared with wide eyes. It read:

Saturday Dinner – Cooking – Dale

Boil water for dishes – Dale

Wash dishes – Dale

Refill water coolers – Dale

Sunday Morning - Get up early and build fire – Dale

Boil water for adults to have coffee – Dale

Wash communal dishes – Dale

Pack trailer – Dale

"Nice of you to sign up for all that so the rest of us can play," said the patrol leader, slapping Dale on the back. Dale sagged as he stood. His head sank, his shoulders drooped, and he slouched off to start on dinner.

Dale was very quiet that evening. About the only times he spoke were to say "yes" or "no", and when he saw to it that Mark got an extra helping of dessert. The kid wasn't any less annoying, but Dale knew that he owed him – big time.

The fog rolled into camp from the lake while the boys were sitting around the campfire. Dale didn't participate in any skits and was quiet during the silly songs. He went to bed before cracker-barrel, just wishing for the weekend to be over so that he could get away from that place and the Devil that was after him.

That night again, Dale was woken at 3:00 a.m. by the raucous squawking of the turkey vultures in their nest. Again he couldn't sleep and, knowing that he would have to face his tormentor, he pulled on some clothes, slipped out of the tent, and walked slowly through the knee-high fog to the fire pit. There, again, was Cypher. Now, he stood about six feet tall and his eyes glowed a dull red in the light of the fire that re-kindled itself in response to a wave of his hand.

"Good evening, Dale," he said, in a strained but civilized tone.

"Good evening," Dale mumbled in reply.

"We had a deal. You have broken faith with me, and I cannot stand for that."

"You'd better undo the merit badges then," said Dale. "The deal's off as far as I'm concerned. I'm not hurting anyone for you."

"Hmm…." the Devil said. "It's not quite that simple, you see. I can change the future, but I cannot change the past. I also cannot leave a deal uneven. Do you understand what that means, young man?"

"Uh, not really," replied Dale.

All trace of decency and respect disappeared from the Devil's voice at this point. "Since you are a coward and a dolt I shall explain it in simple terms. Because I have done more requested things for you than you have done for me, I must do some evil things TO you in order to even the score. Only in that way can our deal be settled." The red eyes gazed into Dale's. "Unless, of course, you want to reconsider?"

Dale thought about it for a few seconds, then pulled himself up straight and looked the Devil in the eye. "No," he said with a calm that surprised him. "I'll take the Devil's vengeance before I become the Devil's servant."

"Very biblical," Cypher sneered at him. "So be it." And, with that, he stalked off through the fog towards the lake.

This time the fire kept burning in the fire ring after the Devil left. Dale looked around for a fire bucket, but they were both empty. With a rueful grin on his face, he fetched the water coolers that he'd filled after dinner and emptied them onto the fire to douse it. He'd fill them up again in the morning. "That's a little redemption right there," he told himself. "I'm a scout at heart after all."

On Sunday morning, Dale built a fire. He got two slivers in his hands as he handled the firewood, but both came out with tweezers from the medical kit. He filled the coolers, and slopped water all down his pants carrying them back to camp. He boiled water for the adults, burning his finger-tips on the stove in the process. And he cleaned up after breakfast, scalding his hands in the hot water for the wash. By the time he was ready to pack the trailer he was just waiting for the next painful disaster.

The process went remarkably well. Mark, who seemed to have appointed himself as Dale's shadow, was there to help all the time. All the gear fit in just fine and nothing fell on him, no matter how high he piled it. With the loading process complete and the last of the boys piling into cars, Dale was beginning to think that maybe his debt to the Devil was paid. That was when the scoutmaster closed the trailer door on his left hand.

Baraboo Memorial Hospital is only a short drive from Devil's Lake State Park. The doctors and nurses at the E.R. were very kind to Dale as they splinted and taped his fingers. Only two were broken, but the ER doctor, with that sense of humor that is so unique to emergency room personnel, assured Dale that the bruising would hurt at least as much as the breaks when the pain-killers wore off.

The SM sent Dale on ahead to his truck while he signed the discharge forms. As Dale approached the truck, the door of the black Lincoln next to it opened, and a familiar figure in a business suit stepped out and removed his sunglasses.

"The deal is done and the score is settled," he said. And so saying, he pulled the contract Dale had signed out of his pocket and tore it in half. The Devil got back into his car and his driver, unseen behind darkened windows, backed out of the parking space and drove off out of the parking lot.

"Who were you talking to?" the SM asked, walking up to the truck.

"Just a guy wanting directions to the park," Dale replied.

As they started homeward the SM coughed gently and said, "Oh, by the way Dale, about that scoutmaster conference for Star...."

"Yes?" Dale replied eagerly.

"I'm afraid there was a slight mistake. It's Dave who has all his requirements done. I must have heard wrong when the Advancement Chair told me."

I won't tell you what went through Dale's mind at that moment. Let's just say that if I were to write it down I'd have use asterisks and exclamation marks to keep it G-rated.

Dale snoozed as he rode home and contemplated how his weekend had turned out. Nobody but him actually got hurt, and since he was left-handed, he wasn't going to have to do chores or written homework for at least four weeks. He had been drawn into a deal with the Devil, and certainly come off the worse for it. In that respect, he did not feel especially proud of himself. But when it really mattered, he had been true to the scout promise. When you looked at it all in balance, he could live with the way things turned out.

7 The Church Basement

Author's Note

This story was written for a specific trip that our troop took in 2010. The boys more or less demanded a story that was about them. This story could be used on any road-trip that a youth group takes where you stay in a church for a night along the way. Fill it with your own kids and leaders as you tell it.

St. John's Lutheran Church was a medium size brick building. It stood slightly to the side of the middle of a quarter section of land in southern Ohio. Around the church was a graveyard with headstones that were, in many cases, clearly older than the church itself. The church land was surrounded by housing subdivisions, and the front quarter was taken up by a parking lot. You could easily imagine how the church must have been built out in the country outside town when it was founded, and in the intervening years the town had grown up and out around it.

The foundation stone by the church door had the date 1956 chiseled into it, and it was more or less exactly what you would expect of a church built in that era. The sanctuary was a rectangle with a roof that was three stories tall. An L-shaped single story building branched off the side of it, containing the church office, bathrooms, a modern kitchen and a couple of meeting rooms for Sunday School and adult classes. The sanctuary was raised a couple of feet above ground level, and the basement walls that were exposed had sliding windows that let light into the full basement under the sanctuary.

It was in that basement that the boys of Troop 628 were scheduled to spend the night. They were traveling home from the National Jamboree and Camp Brady Saunders in Virginia, and the pastor of their own sponsoring church had arranged for them to stay in the church of an old friend from seminary, who now led the congregation at St. John's.

They arrived late – it was almost 8 p.m. – and were met by an elderly caretaker who let them into the church and led them down the stairs and into the basement. The stairway was lined with photographs and press clippings that told the history of the church. The original wooden building had been constructed by settlers in 1832. That structure had stood until 1912, when it burned down after a lightning strike and was replaced with another wooden structure built on the same foundation. A second fire had started in the electrical wiring in November of 1955, again burning the church to the ground. By that time, the congregation had grown to the point that it really needed a larger building, so the church council decided to build a modern brick structure, with a larger sanctuary adjacent to the original sanctuary site. The foundation of the old church would be filled in and the support building constructed on top of it.

There was one rather large difficulty with this plan, however. The church graveyard surrounded the old building on both sides as well as behind. In order to dig the foundation for the new sanctuary, they were going to have to disinter and re-bury forty-two coffins, many of them belonging to the very people who had founded the church some 120 years before. There being no other option, this was done. The founders' remains and head-stones were laid to rest once more in a new plot in the church-yard. Now, however, rather than being next to the church, they were a hundred yards away. A pleasant garden with a fountain and some benches was constructed next to the relocated graves, and the congregation was very diligent about tending the bedding plants in summer and providing fresh flowers at regular intervals during the winter months. It seemed the least that they could do after subjecting them to such an indignity.

Unfortunately, as often happens when one starts digging in an ancient graveyard, it turned out that there were more bodies than headstones in that oldest part of the, uh… "plot". Some of them were buried between the marked graves; some were buried in the same plots, right on top of the coffins of the proper owners of the plot. Many of them weren't even in coffins. Digging with a back-hoe, a number of these unmarked skeletons were "disturbed", which is a nice way of saying that they were torn up a lot, in the process. The workers did their best to keep each set of remains together, but in the end, the best they could do was to assemble twelve sets of unidentified remains, half of which were the skeletons of children, which they reburied, side by side, in a single mass grave at the back corner of the cemetery.

Andrew, who, as troop historian, was in charge of the troop's notice-board, was most interested in the pictures and stories that told the history of St. John's. He lingered behind the group to read, and by the time that he joined them in the basement all the other boys had already claimed space on the floor, leaving him to sleep nearer to the adults than he would have chosen to.

The caretaker was explaining some things to the adults and, as acting SPL, Andrew quickly got into that group so that he could hear what was going on. The caretaker told them where the bathrooms were, that the sanctuary was off-limits, and what time they were expected to be out in the morning.

As he finished up, he turned to Andrew, looked him hard in the eye and said, "And if any of *them* turn up, don't speak to them. You'll only encourage them. There's some folk round here as 'll tell ye they's up and walkin' about most nights. Utter nonsense if you ask me, but you still won't catch me talking to 'em." With that, he shook hands with the adults, turned on his heel and tromped out of the basement, up the stairs, and was heard departing in his car.

The leaders ordered pizza. Rather than have his scouts go running around getting into trouble, Andrew gathered them together and told them the story of the unexpected bodies in the unmarked graves. He did his best to spin it out, getting some of the more imaginative boys to make suggestions as to who they might have been, how they might have died, and why half of them were children. Dane thought that they might have been Indians who died of European diseases, and that the people felt guilty, wanting to give them proper Christian burials but had to do it in secret because the pastor at the time wouldn't have heathens buried in his church yard. Sam said that the dead were thieves who were caught and lynched by the townsfolk, then buried in the churchyard in secret, both to salve the lynch-mobs' conscience and to hide the evidence. Nick said that they were probably all killed by medical students who wanted to dissect their bodies as homework for their medical exams. He was willing to bet that if anyone had counted all the bones, some would have come up missing.

Andrew's strategy worked. The boys sat around thinking up ever more gruesome stories for the un-named dead until the pizza was delivered. Then they demolished the pizza and lay around groaning and complaining that they had all eaten too much, too fast. By this point it was 9:30 and it was pitch dark outside. Mr. Nichols suggested that everybody should go outside and play some flashlight hide and seek around the church-yard to burn off energy and help to settle them down for the night. Andrew joined Nick's patrol to even up the numbers, and they went out with a two minute head start to find their hiding places. The night was clear, and a crescent moon added to the stars and the light pollution of the surrounding town to cast long, dim shadows around the church-yard. Dakota and Levi headed off together to try to find the mass grave they'd been told about. Surely nobody would look for them there. Dane chose to stay right close to the church, hiding among the shadows by the building. The seekers were sure to run right past him, searching the yard before looking close by. Nick and Andrew went their own ways, out into the grave-yard. Nick lay in a shadow behind a mausoleum. Andrew crouched behind a headstone that marked the graves of an entire family.

Justin and Harry's patrol stormed out to search. They didn't worry about night vision, instead turning their flashlights every way, looking for their quarry.

In the darkest corner of the church-yard, Levi and Dakota were hunkered down behind the modest sandstone marker that told the story of the dozen un-named dead. There was no garden here, no flowers to worry about trampling in the dark, nothing but medium length grass and a line of old trees in the back corner of the lot. They had their eyes fixed on the flashlights of the seekers as they fanned out from the church when a girl's voice behind them whispered, "What are you doing?"

They both whipped around to see who had spoken and at first saw nothing but pinpoints of light in front of their eyes where the flashlights had been. As their eyes adjusted, however, they saw a pale head sticking out of the ground about eight feet away from them.

"Are you hiding from somebody?" the head asked. A pair of arms came up out of the ground, pressed down on it, and out popped a full body, glowing palely in the moonlight. The child was dressed in boy's clothes, but had long hair and the voice was definitely a girl. Dakota and Levi were frozen in fright. The girl didn't get up on her feet, but crawled over to them instead, keeping low so that the seekers wouldn't see her. "Can't you talk?" she asked them, as she came close.

Now Levi and Dakota were pretty confused. The ghost girl looked perfectly "normal". She had a nice smile under her unkempt hair and ragged overalls, and she was acting friendly. Levi, who is seldom at a loss for words, stammered out, "W-w-we can talk."

"Is somebody trying to hurt you or are you just playing?" she asked.

"We're just playing hide and seek," Dakota whispered, snapping out of his fright. "Where did you come from?"

"Well, I used to be from over there," she pointed at the church, "but now I'm from over here." She pointed at the ground behind her with her thumb and laughed softly at her own joke.

The flashlights of the seekers were getting closer now. "They're going to catch you soon," the girl remarked. "I could help you to hide better, if you want."

"Where?" both boys asked at once.

"Underground," she replied with a sweet smile. "There are lots of us down there; you'd have plenty of company and *they'd* never find you."

The boys looked at each other for a moment, then Levi said, "Uh, we're still alive. We won't stay that way underground."

The girl looked shocked. "Oh," she said. "Sorry. I.... I haven't seen anyone alive out here since they woke me up with that digging machine." She seemed to pause for a moment, then she said, "Oh well. My name's Meg. Maybe I'll see you again, but I should go and tell the others about you. You really shouldn't be out here you know. A graveyard's the wrong place for the living."

With that, the girl, Meg, sank into the ground and disappeared. The boys breathed a shared sigh of relief, then let out a shared squeak of fright as a hand shot out of the ground where Meg had been, waved at them, and then vanished with the sound of a faint giggle.

Alex and Justin had been pretty close when Dakota and Levi squeaked, and both came running over when they heard it. They shone their flashlights in the boys' eyes and said, "Found ya. What are you squeaking for? Seen a ghost?"

Well, Dakota and Levi told Justin and Alex exactly what they had seen. Not that either Justin or Alex believed a word of it, but they did have a good time teasing the other two as they walked back to the church. Alex literally fell over Andrew as he cut behind a headstone, and before the group of five made it back to the church, shouts of "Found ya!" rose from next to the church and behind a marble crypt as Dane and Nick, too, were discovered.

Regrouping at the church door, Levi began excitedly telling everyone who would listen about Meg the ghost from the mass grave. All the other boys gave him a hard time and he quickly dropped the topic, saying, "Okay, YOU go out there and hide in the dark then!"

It was now Justin's patrol's turn to hide. Each boy went his own way. Harry headed to the parking lot and hid behind one of the vans. No force on earth was going to get him anywhere near that mass grave. Alex, being bigger than anyone else, had the greatest challenge to hide himself, and ended up lying in a shadow behind a large crypt with his knees pulled up to his chest. Justin went to the founders' garden and hid behind a big headstone, but Kanu and Sam wandered about looking for the perfect spot. Eventually, they bumped into one another in the back corner of the graveyard. They were in a largish, grassy area next to a line of trees with a single headstone. Sam flipped on his flashlight with his hand over the lens and opened his fingers just enough to let light onto the stone to read it. "Here lie the remains of twelve unfortunate people of this town who were buried in unmarked spots in this churchyard at some time in the 1800s and relocated to this field in 1956. May God have mercy on their souls," Sam read.

"Quick, behind the headstone. They're coming," said Kanu, and the two of them dropped into the grass exactly where Levi and Dakota had hidden a few minutes before.

"Didn't Meg tell you that this is no place for the living?" a sarcastic voice spoke from behind them.

Now Sam and Kanu aren't stupid, and it took each of them about a millisecond to figure out what this meant. They turned together, seeing each other's horror stricken faces as they passed, and saw, sitting Indian fashion on the grass behind them, a boy of about fifteen. He was a pale figure, just as Levi and Dakota had described Meg. "Hmm," said the boy, "you two look bigger than the ones Meg told us about. Didn't you listen to your friends? The living never do, do you?"

Sam stammered out, "W-w-w-we didn't believe them. We thought they were just trying to scare us."

"Trying to scare you?" The boy was smiling and spoke in a mocking tone. "Oh no, they weren't trying to scare you." His expression hardened and the tone of his voice dropped. "That's my job," he said. At this, he stood up and drew a knife from a sheath on his belt.

Kanu and Sam bolted. They tripped, fell, got up, ran, tripped, fell, got up and ran again. The boy's mocking laughter followed them, but when Kanu looked over his shoulder, he saw the ghostly glow in the field, not following them.

Of course, Sam and Kanu were found by the seekers almost at once. They told about the ghost, and everyone yelled "game over, everyone come in" until the last scout came back to the church door. They all went down to the basement together and collapsed in a circle. Andrew asked each pair of boys who had seen the ghosts to re-tell his story from start to finish, which they did. If you could have seen the faces of the adults you would have laughed. Every one of them was grinning from ear to ear by the time Kanu and Sam finished up. Mr. Obright and Mr. Nichols had been whispering to one another, and now Mr. Nichols said, "I think you boys have been listening to too many of Mr. Bain's stories." Mrs. Christensen simply shook her head and said, "I think it's time everyone brushed their teeth and went to bed. You should tell your tale to Mr. Bain when we get home, maybe he can use for a campfire story some day."

"But it's true. There really are ghosts out there in the graveyard!" Dakota insisted, with Levi, Sam and Kanu nodding vigorously in agreement.

"Perhaps so," said Mr. Nichols, "but the ghosts are out there, not in here, so get ready for bed and get some sleep. We have a long drive ahead of us tomorrow."

There was a lot of grumbling, but the scouts did as they were told and bedded down for the night. The adults did likewise, and soon the only sound to be heard in the basement was gentle snoring from the adult end of the room.

Mr. Obright woke up at some early hour and tried to shift into a better position to get back to sleep. He heard soft conversation from the scouts' end of the room, and lifted his head to see if anyone was up and in need of shushing. What he saw left him feeling cold. There were more than ten figures lying at the other end of the room, and several softly glowing adults were standing looking at the sleeping figures, quietly discussing something. Mr. Obright slipped out of his sleeping bag and stood up. One of the glowing figures waved to him, motioning him over to his group. There didn't seem to be any threat in it, so Mr. Obright walked over carefully. The huddle of adults consisted of four men and two women. On the floor in front of them, were the curled-up figures of the ten scouts plus six gently glowing figures of other children, lying between the scouts, asleep in their clothes without sleeping pads or bags.

"It's a funny thing, that," remarked one of the men. "Fifty-four years and not a wink of sleep for one of them young'uns, and now look at 'em. All it takes is bunch of kids in *their* proper place, and they're all sleepin' like babies."

"Keep your voice down, Jeb," whispered a woman. She looked straight at Mr. Obright. "An' tha' goes for you too. If one of them livin' kids wakes up and sees our lot in among 'em he'll yell the place down."

Now Mr. Obright is pretty good at rolling with punches. He motioned the adults off to a corner and pointed at some chairs, sitting down himself.

"Can't," whispered the second woman. "We go right through, see?" and she swung a leg through the chair.

"Oh," said Mr. Obright, "I see." At this, he sat on the floor, and the ghosts joined him in like fashion.

"I assume that you are the twelve whose graves weren't marked?" he asked.

"Arr. That's us," replied one of the men.

"Have you had no peace since your graves were moved?" Mr. Obright asked.

"Arr. That's so," came the reply.

"So why are the children at peace now, but you adults are not?"

"Your boys took notice of Meg and Abe," said the man named Jeb. "Ain't nobody paid 'em no attention since before they was buried. All any of us needs is for people to pay us a little attention. Just like them "founders" with their garden and their flowers. We don't see them walking the yard at night, sleepless and wanderin'."

Mr. Obright understood. All these waking spirits needed was a little recognition - somebody to remember them and pay them some respect. If they had that, they'd be able to rest at peace. He asked the group, "Who are you, and how did you come to buried in unmarked plots?"

"It's not what you might think," replied one of the women. "We was all on the trail out west, California for me and my man. It's a long trek, and accidents or disease happened a lot. If somebody got sick or hurt on the trail, they'd be brought to the nearest town. Pastor Franke and his wife, they was good souls. Ministered to body as well as spirit. Didn't care who you were they didn't.

"Now the townspeople, they weren't all as kind. Didn't want them that died in *their* graveyard. But Pastor Franke, he wasn't having none of that. He dug the graves in his churchyard himself. Put us among or on top of all the high-and-mighty of the town and said proper words over us before he filled in the dirt. None of 'em ever guessed or knew it was rocks in the coffins he gave to the sheriff to bury in the unmarked pauper's graves outside of town."

At this, all six ghosts chuckled and nodded. "We slept right fine where Pastor Franke laid us," added one of the men.

"And then the descendants of those *high and mighty* towns-folk dug you up and put you in a common grave on the edge of their cemetery?" Mr. Obright asked.

"Arr. Dug us up with a machine. Broke our bodies, and put us all in the same hole," came the reply.

"I reckon as we may as well try to get some sleep too, seein' as this kind gentleman has heard our story and been good enough to pay us some heed. Go you and sleep some more, kind sir, and we'll try an' do the same. Oh, an' sir. See if you can roll that big one over as you pass. 'Is snorin' 'd wake the dead!" Even Mr. Obright chuckled at that, and he did indeed give Mr. Nichols a nudge as he passed, causing him to shift in his sleep and quiet his breathing.

Soon all was quiet in the basement of St. John's church, and morning sunlight was arcing into the room when Mr. Obright awoke. He told the story of his night-time "chat" to the other adults, and then to the patrol leaders. It was Sunday morning, but Home Depot opens early on Sundays, even in Ohio, so Mr. Obright took the four boys who had seen the ghosts shopping for plants and shrubs that morning before service.

At the service, the troop was introduced, and Mr. Obright was given the chance to address the congregation. He told the portion of the story of the relocated graves as it was recounted in the history of the church in the basement stair, and said that everyone in the troop was grateful to have slept in their basement – in the same space that once had housed these unknowns. As a thank-you, the troop proposed to plant bushes and perennial flowers on the bare plot where the twelve now lay. He asked that the St. John's youth group take charge of maintaining the garden, and the youth pastor assured him that they would.

After the service, the boys of Troop 628 set up their garden in the plot at the back of the cemetery, then they washed up, piled into the vans and headed on their way.

The last time the troop committee chair talked to the pastor of 628's sponsor church, the pastor passed along the thanks of his old friend for the gardening that the troop had done when it stayed in his church. He was concerned, however, that the boys might have been rather wild when they stayed. Apparently his friend had told him that things were much quieter in the churchyard *after* the troop had left.

8 The Demon Troop

Chad and Simon were second year scouts in our Troop. Both were unable to go to EBSR summer camp with their own troop because of family conflicts, so they signed up as provisional campers for a week in July instead.

Simon's dad drove them to camp. When they arrived, they were assigned to be with Troop 966. It was a small troop with only six scouts – two first years, three second years and a high-schooler. The high-schooler served as the SPL. He had collar length, wavy hair and was named David. What was kind of creepy, though, was that all the others had identical neat, short haircuts – the classic schoolboy style, combed straight forward with straight-cut bangs. Among the second years, there was one pair of identical twins, both of whom wore identical sunglasses.

The scoutmaster was a woman. She was about fifty five years old with black hair, shot with grey. She introduced herself as Miss Tracy and said, "We're all very glad you can join us this week." The ASM was a man who could generously be described as "older than dirt". He introduced himself as Ron.

The scouts of Troop 966 were camping in Mohawk camp. They were incredibly organized. There was little talking, no goofing around, and their camp was neat as a pin.

Five tents were arranged in a perfect circle around the fire-pit with two scouts to a tent.

Miss Tracy had the tent closest to the exit path. The SPL and a second year had the one to her left. The second year twins had the one to her right. The two first years and the two visitors got the tents farthest away. A sixth tent stood some way apart from the rest. This was Ancient Ron's.

Simon asked one of the twins why their scoutmaster was called by her first name. His response was so angry it could almost have been called a bark. "We do not speak her true name," he retorted, getting right into Simon's face. David stepped in quickly and said, "Relax man. It's something Russian and pretty much unpronounceable – that's why she lets us call her Miss Tracy." Still, Simon was a little taken aback.

The scouts of Troop 966 formed a single patrol. Each had an identical patrol patch on his shoulder – a smiling demon holding a spear.

Oddly – the SM also wore a patrol patch. It was a burning eye – much like the eye of Sauron in Lord of the Rings. Chad noticed it first and snickered to Simon that Miss Tracy must be a bit too much of a J. R. R. Tolkien fan. Later, as they waited in line for swim tests, he asked her directly if she was a fan but she replied, "No. But you may be surprised by how much a person can see when she stares into a fire." This seemed a bit cryptic, but Chad brushed it off as Miss Tracy being just another weird adult, of whom there were plenty in his own troop, so it wasn't anything unusual. Troop 966's performance at the swim test was also a bit odd. David's tent-mate wore a backpack which he refused to remove. This meant that he couldn't do the test at all. One first year was already in water shoes when he came down to the beach and never removed them even when he swam. The other was in jeans shorts and also skipped the test. The twins went in, but they just did the beginner test and could do little more than doggy paddle. None of the boys seemed to be all that fond of, or comfortable in, the water. Chad and Simon, however, were both strong swimmers, so they felt pretty good about their performance. Chad had signed up for the mile swim program, so he was going to be spending plenty of time in the water.

David added Chad and Simon to the patrol duty roster and they did their best to learn the routines of the new patrol. They didn't do too badly considering that it was all new.

The Demon Patrol boys were almost frighteningly polite. They all sat straight backed at the table and waited until the adults served themselves before they began to eat. All had perfect manners, and Chad and Simon felt out of place as their heads got ever closer to their plates while they slurped up spaghetti in the dining hall. Miss Tracy glared at them disapprovingly.

That evening the troop built a fire in the campsite but there were no songs, skits or stories. The boys just stared into the fire or looked at their scoutmaster with expectant gazes, as if waiting for her to do something. That wasn't the end of the odd behavior though. The twins never took off their sunglasses, even when it was pitch dark, and David's tent-mate never took off his day-pack.

Time to hit the tents was called at 9:30 and lights-out at 10:00. Other than Chad and Simon, nobody talked after lights-out. Miss Tracy came over, banged on their ridge-pole and told them she was disappointed in their behavior and that she wanted them to be more like the boys in her troop, from whom they could take a few lessons in manners and good behavior. Clearly, this troop was <u>not</u> much like ours!

The next day, Chad and Simon felt kind of bad and tried to do the best they could with breakfast. Chad went with one of the twins to fetch the breakfast stuff. The kid moved incredibly fast. He could jump from branch to hillock as if a ten foot leap were nothing. Chad had trouble keeping up and complemented him on his athletic ability. The boy just grinned from behind his ever-present sunglasses and said it was one of his "talents".

In breakfast prep, the boys worked hard and at the table they put on their best manners to try to please the SM. It worked. After breakfast, as Simon washed up, Mrs. B., the camp director, came to camp to ask the SM how the two provisional campers were settling in. "Great," she replied with a laugh and a smile. "They're working just like demons!"

Merit Badge classes started at 9:00. Simon had signed up for Pioneering, Environmental Science and Rifle. Chad had Mile Swim, Wilderness Survival, and Rifle in the same group with Simon.

Lunch was in the mess-hall. The troop got dinged for Backpack Boy not removing his pack, but other than that the Demon patrol, Chad and Simon included, were models of good manners and behavior. They were learning fast and were pleased when Miss Tracy gave them a big smile at the end of the meal and said that they seemed to be quite at home with her Demons. After lunch they had rifle MB, then drifted back to camp to see what the other guys planned to get up to. To their surprise, all the boys went to their tents to take a nap! "What is this, Kindergarten?" the guys asked each other. The nap example was one that they were categorically not going to follow. Instead, they went down to the water-front and played in the lake until they were good and tired. They got back to camp with their shaggy middle-schooler hair plastered all over their faces. That was when Ancient Ron spoke to them for the first time. "You boys need haircuts," he grumbled, and walked away. Chad and Simon just looked at each other and burst out laughing.

Dinner prep went pretty well. Simon fetched food with the boy who had swum in water-shoes. He seemed to have a little trouble walking properly, so it took a while. Chad helped to cook together with the other first year. The kid was very focused on the task at hand. Try as he might, Chad couldn't get him to talk about anything other than cooking and serving the meal. "Working like a little demon," Chad reminded himself with a wry grin. When they were done cleaning up (which went incredibly fast), the Troop 966 boys all headed off down the road in the direction of the shooting ranges. They didn't ask Chad and Simon to join them, even though the boys asked where they were going. Chad and Simon were a bit hurt by that. After all, they'd been doing their best to fit in. They decided to go to the trading post instead.

When they returned, Miss Tracy was waiting for them with Ron at the fire pit. "You two are fitting in very well," she said. "Perhaps my boys would accept you a little better if you showed them that you want to join us as part of the patrol." She held out two Demon Patrol patches to them.

They looked at each other for a moment before Chad replied, "I'm not sure we're ready for that. We're pretty attached to our own patrol – the Green Knights."

"I understand. But remember, I have the patches if you should change your minds. We'd be thrilled if you would both join us."

Monday evening's campfire was livelier. Rather than singing songs or doing skits, this troop seemed to like to tell scary stories, complete with reenactment. All their stories were about dark creatures and forces that rose up and terrorized campers and other innocent people. Some of it was a bit gory, but Chad and Simon agreed that is was mostly first-rate scary stuff. The first year who had helped Chad to cook dinner also did a ceremonial dance. It looked a lot like the Indian dances Chad and Simon had seen the OA do, but there was something different about it. It was a little wilder, and somehow more violent and less graceful. "Maybe he's still learning," they figured.

At 9:30, Miss Tracy stood up and a hush fell on the camp. "Bedtime again!!??" Chad and Simon were thinking, but instead she announced "Night Games". The 966 boys let up a cheer and tore off into the woods. David stayed with Chad and Simon and explained the games. First was to be capture the flag, and second was the man-hunt. The two twins would be the prey with the boundaries of camp as the boundaries of the game. The rest of the scouts would split into two hunting parties. The first team to catch either twin, tie him up, and bring him back to Miss Tracy would be the winner. Sounded like fun!

For capture the flag, the boys were on the same team with David and the first year dancer. They got crushed. The other boys seemed to see like cats and move like lightning, especially the twins, who had finally taken off their sunglasses. This, explained David, was why they both serve as prey in the hunt game. If either of them was a hunter they'd catch any other prey in no time.

Chad and Simon were on separate teams for the hunt. David started the game off with a yell of "The Hunt is on!" and the twins disappeared into the woods. Two minutes later, the hunting parties crashed into the woods after them. The hunt lasted until almost 3:00 a.m. when one of the twins (who can tell which??) was caught and dragged back to camp by Simon's team. Then the whole troop fell into bed, exhausted. "That was awesome fun," Chad and Simon agreed, right before they too fell asleep.

Getting up at 6:00 the next morning was NOT fun, however. Chad struggled to do his laps at mile-swim and they stumbled and nodded through their morning classes. Simon spilled his glass of milk at lunch and Chad was lucky not to get thrown out of rifle class because he was waving his rifle barrel around so much as he tried to stay awake and aim at the same time. After that, both Chad and Simon stumbled back to camp and fell into their tent to pass out and nap until dinner, just like the rest of their adopted troop.

Tuesday night went much as Monday had. The dancing boy starred again. He had a really weird gate as he walked and danced, they noticed. They couldn't quite figure out what it was. Simon thought the boy swung his hips like a teenage girl. Chad said it looked like his center of gravity was too far back, and that this gave him a weird balance. That night, the troop skipped capture the flag and went straight to the hunt. Keeping up with the others was as hard as ever, but Chad and Simon were beginning to understand the strategy of the hunt. Each team worked like a wolf pack – spreading wide and closing in on its prey – forcing the prey into a corner or a gully where they could trap it until a hunter could pounce and bring it down.

Wednesday morning was not as bad, thanks to the Tuesday nap, and they made it through Merit Badge classes pretty well. They had begun to talk more with the other scouts. Backpack Boy had even told them his name – it was Travis. The Troop 966 boys had told them both that they should accept the patrol patches Miss Tracy had offered. "Give her your Class A shirt while you're at class and she'll even sew it on for you," Travis had told Simon helpfully.

Chad was scheduled to spend Wednesday night sleeping rough with his Wilderness Survival class. He had to admit that he was a bit disappointed to miss the coming evening with his adopted troop. David had announced that there would be a special ceremony at campfire that night, and all the boys were clearly excited – more emotion than any of them had shown all week as far as Chad was concerned. Chad went off with the Wilderness Survival group at the mid-afternoon break. Before he left, Simon confided in him that he was going to accept and wear the Demon Patrol patch that had been offered. There were only two more full days of camp to go, so Chad figured it wouldn't do any harm and made no effort to talk him out of it.

Chad's night in the woods was a lot quieter than the last two he'd spent racing through it on the hunt. They found a very limited supply of edible plants and berries, and Chad was really hungry as he tried to get to sleep on his bed of ferns, leaves and small branches. Noise from the "ceremony" – chanting, roaring, whooping and hollering – could be heard dimly drifting across the camp.

It wasn't much of a night's sleep. The bugs, both flying and crawling, kept disturbing Chad. He hiked back to Mohawk camp at dawn and crawled into his tent to try to get a couple of hours' worth of sleep before breakfast.

When David woke them up at 6:30 Chad asked Simon about the ceremony. "It was wild. They really welcomed me into their troop. I'm one of them now," Simon replied.

"Really?" Chad asked. "Like you're going to stay in this troop even after we go home?"

"If I can, yes," came the reply. "You should too. Look how much fun the night games are, and the scary stories everyone tells at campfire. Miss Tracy" (he said it more like "Mistress E") "is an awesome scoutmaster, and the ceremony – you have to go through the ceremony. You have to join us." This last phrase was spoken in a voice that almost wasn't Simon's. The way he stressed each sound in the words sounded more like Miss Tracy than Simon, and the way he called her "Mistress E" was just plain weird.

"I'll think about it," Chad said.

The two started to get dressed for morning flag. Neither of them could find their Class A shirts, however, and though it seemed out of character for the other boys to do such a thing (they were usually such a polite, considerate bunch) Chad quickly concluded that the Troop 966 guys must have taken them. He crawled out of the tent to go and find David or Miss Tracy to complain, but as he stood up, Miss Tracy approached him, carrying the two shirts. "I hope you don't mind," she said with a huge grin, "but since Simon went through the ceremony last night, and we're hoping you will tonight, I took the liberty of sewing your Demon Patrol patch on too."

"Oh," was all Chad could say at first. It would have been really rude to say, "Yes, I do mind. Go take it off and put my Green Knight back on there right now!" Instead, all he managed was, "Um, thanks, I guess."

"Will you join us in the ceremony tonight?" Miss Tracy pressed him.

"I still don't know. I'll think about it."

Miss Tracy wouldn't let it go. "Simon loved the ceremony," she said. "Ask him about it. I'll tell David to plan for another ceremony tonight. That way everything will be ready." And with that, she turned and walked off to talk to David without giving Chad a chance to reply. David turned to Chad and gave him two thumbs up after Miss Tracy finished speaking to him, then the whole troop fell in and marched off to Flag.

Mrs. B. was up at Flag early as the troops marched in. "I see you boys are really fitting in well with 966," she said, seeing their matching patrol patches.

"Yes Ma'ám," Simon replied with a smile. Chad just looked at his shoes and kept walking.

Chad's second MB class ran late, and he was the last one to return to camp for lunch. As he came in, he heard an odd buzzing noise, and was stunned to find Simon sitting in a camp chair with a sheet wrapped round his shoulders, and Ancient Ron cutting his hair with a trimmer and comb. "Used to be a barber when I was young," Ron mumbled as Chad walked up. "You next?"

"Uh-uh, no way," replied Chad.

"Hmm. Maybe tomorrow," mumbled Ron. Simon stood up from the chair and admired himself in the mirror Ron handed him. He now sported the exact same haircut as all the other Troop 966 boys. "Now I'm really one of the Demons. Chad, you *have* to join us in the ceremony tonight."

"Not if I have to get that haircut I don't," said Chad.

"You don't have to, but you'll want to. You'll see," was Simon's reply as he walked off to check the duty roster for lunch.

Rifle went well that Thursday. Both Simon and Chad were very close to qualifying scores and they were sure that they'd get what they needed to complete the requirements the next day. During afternoon free time, David advised them both to catch a nap. The ceremony would go pretty late. Simon nodded enthusiastically and led Chad into the tent to lie down. Chad didn't sleep, however. He was tired, but he lay there trying to figure out how to get out of doing the ceremony without offending anyone. He was pretty sure everyone from Simon to Miss Tracy would be really ticked off if he told them he wasn't interested. In the end, he did what most twelve-year-olds will do under such circumstances. He put off the decision and decided to wing it.

The ceremony began at sundown with a fire being built and lit. The boys all came out of their tents and sat in front of them, Indian fashion. All were perfectly orderly, perfectly still. All were wearing Class A for the ceremony.

David used a stick to draw a single line from the mouth of Miss Tracy's tent to mouth of the tent two to its clockwise side. He worked his way around the circle of tents until he had drawn a five pointed star, a pentagram, around the fire-pit and to each tent door. As David connected the final line of the pentagram, the fire burned brighter and higher and the 9s on the Demon Patrol's uniform shirts begin to blur and turn. In a matter of a few seconds, the boys of Troop 966 became the boys of Troop 666. Miss Tracy stepped into the circle at the center of the pentagram and held both hands to the sky, then threw them down toward the fire. "Rise!" she shouted. "Rise Master and rise Demons as we celebrate the rite of joining!" A flash of flame shot out of the fire and from it stepped something red and burning.

The thing that stepped from the fire was about four feet tall. It had four muscle-bound arms, each of which ended in a twelve-clawed hand. Its eyes were lifeless black holes and the rows of shark teeth in its mouth dripped with blood and lava. It was a demon from the 7th level of hell, and it wasn't pretty.

"Show yourselves and show your marks," Miss Tracy commanded.

Simon leaned over to Chad and whispered, "Each of us bears our Demon's mark, sssseee." At this, Simon turned his flash light on to show his tongue sticking out from between his lips. It was long and forked like a snake's. "I can't wait to ssssee what yoursss will be," he added.

Chad was beginning to freak. He looked around the circle. To his and Simon's right, the two first years were standing. Dancing Boy had pulled off his shorts and begun to dance. Behind him waived a four foot long tail that he used to balance as he pulled off complex dance moves. The other kid, the one who walked kind of slow, had his sneakers and socks off. Each of his feet ended in a cloven hoof. The twins had their glasses off again, but now that their faces were lit by the fire, Chad saw that both had yellow wolves' eyes, staring hungrily at him. One of them raised a hairy hand with an impossibly long, claw-like finger nail, inserted it into his nostril, pulled out an enormous booger and flicked it into the fire – causing howls of laughter from his twin and the other Demon Patrol boys. Travis stood then and, reaching behind him, pulled his backpack off. As he did so, a pair of bat wings emerged from it. He stretched them out – fully 6 feet on each side of his body and stood with his arms folded, staring at Chad. Last to show his mark was David, the SPL. He pushed the wavy hair back from his face to reveal two small horns atop his head. Dancing Boy yelled out, "Didn't you guess, Chad? He's a teenager – always horny!" This brought another round of laughter from the Demon boys.

Last of all, Chad's eyes fell on Miss Tracy and Ron. Ron was now bent over, a hump clearly visible on his back. Miss Tracy, standing next to the fire inside the pentagram, held out her hands to Chad as a mother would when inviting a child to receive a hug. She gave him a big smile that clearly showed her fangs and said, "Step into the ring. Step into the ring, let your Demon possess you, feel his strength, share his talents, live forever and be a lord among men. It only hurts for a moment and then you will revel in your new power. Join us!"

"Join us, join us, join us, join us," the boys picked up the chant. Chad felt Simon's hand in his back urging him forward into the pentagon ring inside the pentagram star. The other boys started to raise their hands at the sides, forming a ring that would bar Chad's escape. "Join us, join us, join us." The Demon Troop's chant filled Chad's ears, Miss Tracy's arms beckoned him into her embrace and the unspeakable thing that stood in the fire motioned him forward with all the claws on its arms.

With only a second to act, and Simon's hand at his back, Chad made up his mind. He ran forward, bursting through the line of arms between Travis the bat boy and the kid with the hooves. He headed out onto the camp road and ran as if the demons were after him which, of course, they were.

"The Hunt is on," a voice called from behind. "At least give him a head start. Otherwise there's no sport in it." That was David's voice.

Chad ran along the road toward Chippewa camp, trying to decide where to run, where to hide. He saw the sign for the swimming beach in the star-light and that gave him the idea. The demon boys hadn't been comfortable in the water. "Hellfire and water don't mix well, I guess," he thought to himself.

Chad took the beach road. At the beach, he climbed the fence, ripped off his uniform shirt, buttons popping everywhere, pulled off his sneakers, ran out on the dock, dived straight off the end and struck out strongly for the far shore of the lake. He hoped that Simon would be as repulsed by the water as the other demon boys now that he had joined them. Simon wasn't as strong a swimmer as Chad, but Chad could do without the pressure.

Chad got into a rhythm, one breath every three strokes, switch to breast stroke every tenth breath and check that he was still heading for the lights of the far shore, then back to crawl again. It was as he was checking his direction this way that something hit him in the back and pushed him under water. He came up spluttering and spitting water from his mouth. He treaded water for a moment, looked around and was hit hard in the side of the head by a sneaker. Chad went under again in his surprise, but when he came up, he immediately took a deep breath and dived below the surface to give himself a few seconds to think. Who or what could be kicking him from the air in the middle of Castle Rock Lake? Of course, it had to be Travis the bat boy. Chad surfaced on his back and looked up at the star-filled sky. Sure enough, soaring in circles above him was a black shape with bat wings, blocking out the Milky Way as it passed. Travis dove again, but this time Chad was ready for the attack. He swam a resting back stroke, and as Travis stalled his dive above the water to land his kick, Chad grabbed his foot and pulled him into the lake. A hiss of steam rose from the water as Travis splashed down. His flimsy bat wings were a real hindrance in the water, and Chad, the stronger swimmer by far, was able to land several good punches on Travis' face before he broke off and left Travis struggling to get enough air under his wings to take off again.

Chad saw no more of Travis as he swam, and after twenty minutes of swimming back stroke and searching the sky, he turned back to his front and powered on towards the eastern shore.

When he reached the shore, Chad took a minute or two to rest and catch his breath. Would Travis have made it back to EBSR? Did he tell the other Demon Scouts that Chad was swimming before coming to make his attack? How long would it take the wolf twins to run around the south end of the lake and smell him out?

He headed for the first lights he saw. It proved to be medium sized travel-trailer. A middle aged couple was sitting outside sipping their drinks when Chad burst into the light of their lantern. The woman let out a little shriek and the man immediately stepped up and stood between his wife and Chad. "What's going on?" he asked. His voice showed that he was clearly angry.

"I'm sorry, sir," Chad puffed. "Awful things are chasing me. I just swam across the lake to get away. I need your help."

The man's face softened and his wife got up and stood beside him. "Swam across the lake! You must be exhausted. Sit down at the picnic table and have a drink," she said. The woman poured Chad a glass of lemonade and pulled some baked bars out of a cooler. Chad sucked down the lemonade and demolished the dessert as the people looked on.

When he finished and looked up, the couple was watching him intently. "Now, how about you tell us who's after you?"

So Chad gave them the brief version of the story. He ended by asking how far it was back to EBSR by road and estimating that the wolf brothers would take about two hours to get there on foot, meaning that they would be there pretty soon.

"I think you have too much imagination, boy," the man said. "But something's obviously scared you pretty well. I'm going to call the sheriff and turn you over to him."

Twenty minutes later, Chad was in the back seat of a police cruiser wearing an "Adams County Sheriff Department" T-shirt, and on his way back to camp. They got back to EBSR at 12:30 a.m. Mrs. B. was, to say the least, not amused. She had been through a complete "lost camper" drill and had her entire staff out searching every corner of the camp for half the night. She wasn't buying Chad's story at all. Chad was kept at the Camp Ranger's house while Miss Tracy was summoned. He was really nervous to see her again, but when she showed up (fangless!) she put on a show of great concern. Her version of the story ran like this....

Chad had gone into his tent for a nap after his afternoon Merit Badge sessions. He had slept all through dinner, and they had left him to sleep, knowing that he wouldn't have slept much on his Wilderness Survival overnight, and also knowing how much he enjoyed the troop's night games. When Simon went to wake him at 9:00 so that he could join the camp-fire program, Chad had gone berserk. He had run out of his tent yelling that the boys were all demons, attacked Travis when Travis tried to hold him and calm him down, then sprinted off out of the camp and disappeared. The best she could guess, Chad had been having nightmares based on the fire-side stories her boys had told earlier in the week. When he'd been woken from one of them, it had seemed so real that he thought he was living it.

You don't have to have spent too much time around adults to figure out whose story Mrs. B. believed. Chad was told to go back to his tent, get some sleep, and they would call his dad in the morning to come and take him home. He refused point blank. No force on earth was going to get him back into that campsite. SO.... Mrs. B. called his dad then and there, at 1:30 a.m. and told him to come and fetch his son, who had had a nightmare, beaten up another scout, and run away from camp. Chad cringed as he listened to the EBSR end of the conversation.

Dawn was breaking when Chad's father arrived at camp. He was <u>not</u> in a good mood. Chad told him his version of the previous night's events but he just shook his head in disbelief, then actually *apologized* to Mrs. B. and to Miss Tracy for all the trouble Chad had caused. He also insisted that they go back to Mohawk campsite to fetch Chad's gear. Chad was not keen, but his dad clamped his hand on the back of Chad's neck and steered him in the appropriate direction in the way that parents do when they're telling you, "You messed up, I'm making the decisions now, and we're going this way." Back at camp, Miss Tracy woke the other boys up. She had Simon pack up Chad's things while Chad's dad forced him to apologize to the other boys in Troop 966, one at a time. The weird thing was, none of them had the deformities of the previous night now. David was horn-free, Dancing Boy and his tent-mate stood in shorts and bare feet – neither a tail nor a hoof to be seen, and the wolf twins had gentle, hazel-brown eyes. Travis had no backpack, but he did have one black eye, a split, swollen lip and a swollen ear. Simon shot looks at Chad that were a mixture of sympathy, embarrassment and pure hatred. The Demon Patrol members either said nothing as Chad gave his forced apology, or mumbled "apology accepted". Apologizing to Miss Tracy was the worst. She handed him back his Class A shirt, which now had the green knight back on the shoulder and all the buttons attached as if he had never ripped them off. She even gave him a sweet, condescending smile as she said that she was sorry that things had worked out as they had, especially after Chad had seemed to be fitting in so well. Chad mumbled his apology to her too, and then his dad hefted Chad's duffle bag, gave one last "I'm so sorry for the trouble my son caused," and led Chad off down the road in the direction of the parking lot, with Simon in tow carrying Chad's sleeping bag and sleeping mat. Chad was not even permitted the dignity of carrying his own gear.

By this point, Chad was beginning to wonder about his own story. When you thought about it, it was kind of crazy. Could he have dreamed the ceremony and actually gone berserk when they woke him up like Miss Tracy said? That almost did sound more plausible. Chad's dad told him he'd have to ride in the back of the car. He didn't even want to talk to Chad on the way home. He muttered something about needing to call Chad's doctor and make an appointment to have his head examined.

At the parking lot, Chad's dad tossed the bag into the trunk, told Chad to say goodbye to Simon and went around to get into the car. Simon put the rest of Chad's things into the trunk, closed it, and extended a hand to Chad. "Sorry it didn't work out," he said.

Chad took his friend's hand and was about to say, "Yeah, me too," when Simon pressed his hand very hard, winked at him, hissed, "Our master's marks can be hidden, for a while," then slid his forked tongue out of his mouth and licked his lips. Chad ripped his hand free and got into the back right side of the car as Simon smirked at him and ran his fingers over the demon patch on his shoulder.

Chad's dad drove slowly out of camp on the gravel road. He didn't look in the mirror or speak. He was obviously furious. Chad rested his head in his hand and looked out of the side window. Something was running through the woods, keeping pace with the car. At the stop sign at the road, they had to wait for a couple of logging trucks to go past. One of the wolf-twins emerged from the woods while they waited. As the car shook with the roar of the passing eighteen wheeler, he leapt from the woods edge to the car in a single bound, pressed his face against Chad's window, stared at Chad with cold yellow eyes and mouthed the words, "Join us." Then he disappeared from sight as Chad's father pulled out onto County Highway G for the long, silent drive back home.

9 The Ghost of Eckelberry School

The Woodman Center for Camping and Education is one of three camp properties belonging to the Glacier's Edge Council of south central Wisconsin. Woodman Center is named for Joan Woodman, who lived on the land all her life, and donated it to the then Four Lakes Council when she retired to a nursing home.

Mrs. Woodman had a rather unusual hobby. She collected one-room school houses! There are quite a few of them on the property. Many are equipped with bunks and kitchens. Some even have heat. Scout troops can rent them to use as rainy day activity locations or as bunk-houses. There are also several traditional camping sites on the property, both in the valley where most of the school houses are located and up on the hillsides.

One school house, located away up on its own by the entry road, is not used for much of anything, however. If you've ever wondered why it was put away up there out of the way and more or less ignored, the story I will tell you tonight may help to shed some light on the subject.

You see, the Eckelberry School only ever had one teacher. Her name was Miss Hagerman, and she taught in the school for her whole career from 1906 until 1948! Towards the end, the only reason that the district kept Eckelberry School open was to see

Miss Hagerman through to her retirement. She liked to attend school board meetings, and often said that she had put most of her soul into that school. When Miss Hagerman retired, the board closed the school that very summer, and it stood shut up there for twenty years before Joan Woodman bought it and moved it to her valley.

But I promised you a story, not a history lesson. This story is about two scouts from Madison. Mike and Doug were both seventh graders. They were thirteen years old, First Class and Star, respectively, and they loved to camp with their troop. They'd been to the Woodman Center several times already by the October weekend I will tell you about tonight. They had slept in many of the campsites and a couple of the school houses. They'd been inside most of the buildings even when they were cubs and came to the Woodman Center for weekend activity sessions. But, they had never been inside Eckelberry School.

After setting up camp that Friday, there was a little daylight left and their patrol had been granted free time to explore, so Mike and Doug took the scouts on a hike up the hill to look at Eckelberry School. Getting up there, they gave each other a leg up to look in at the windows, but nobody could see very much. The daylight was fading and the windows were dirty and cobwebbed.

After dinner, the boys were all sitting around the campfire when Mike decided to "step into the woods for a moment" to relieve himself. He nudged Doug and said, "I need a buddy. Come on."

So they stepped out of the fire-light and Doug looked around as Mike watered a fallen log. As Doug gazed down the valley he thought he saw a light on the hillside. It was very faint and silvery, but definitely a light. He pointed it out to Mike and said, "There's somebody up in the empty school. Look!"

The two of them watched the school for about five minutes but nobody came out and the faint light stayed. They returned to the fire as the SPL was calling, "Time for bed," so they headed for their tent.

"Whadya say we go and check out that light in the old school?" Doug asked Mike as they zipped up the tent. "We'll just hang out here for twenty minutes then head up there once the adults are asleep."

"What if somebody from one of the other troops sees us?" asked Mike.

"We're a buddy pair. We can be out and about if we want to. There's no reason for anyone to give us a hard time. We'll just say that we're going up to our car to fetch an extra blanket or something," replied Doug.

So, about twenty minutes later, Mike and Doug quietly slipped out of their tent and headed along the road and up the hill towards Eckelberry School. There was no doubting it now that it was 10:30 and all the fires in the valley were out. There was a pale light in that schoolhouse.

Quietly, carefully, they sneaked up to the building. Mike knelt down below one of the tall windows and Doug gently stepped up on his back to peak in. The scene he saw was almost like an old black and white photograph. The window was clean, and inside, lit by a pale light that seemed to come from the very walls and ceiling, stood a woman teacher in an old-fashioned full-length dress. She stood in front of a blackboard. In front of her, were two desks with two boys sitting at them. Both boys were a little younger than Doug and Mike, and both were bent over their desks, writing feverishly.

Mike and Doug decided to make their way around to the main door and have a listen and a peak in to see what was going on. As they took their first careful steps onto the porch of the school, however, the doors of the schoolhouse flew open, and the teacher stood there, lit from behind, glaring at them. From her silvery appearance, and the fact that they could clearly see straight through her, there was no doubting that she was a ghost. "I am Miss Hagerman, and you two are late for school. Come in and take your seats," the ghost said in a commanding voice.

Now the boys had one thing in their hearts and minds at this point – RUN! But somehow they couldn't. There was something in the ghost's voice that they just had to obey. As much as they tried to force themselves to run away, they found themselves walking slowly across the porch and through the doorway of the school. The ghost teacher stood aside to let them by, then firmly closed the door behind them.

Inside the school, two more desks had appeared behind the ones the smaller boys occupied. "School begins at nine," they heard the teacher say from behind them. "You are over an hour and a half late. Lateness is punishable in my school. Face me and hold out your left hands."

The two small boys had turned in their seats to watch, and Mike and Doug saw that they were about ten years old, and dressed in old-fashioned clothes too. Both seemed to be wearing black or brown overalls over button-down shirts, clothes that would have been common a century ago, but had no place on a kid today. Like the teacher they seemed colorless and rather transparent. Ghost students for a ghost teacher.

Once again, there was something in the teacher's voice that they couldn't disobey. Even as they turned and raised their left hands, Mike and Doug saw Miss Hagerman raise a thin bamboo cane. She stood to their side, and brought the cane down sharply on first Mike's hand, then Doug's. Both boys expected it to hurt, but the ghostly cane barely stung at all. "Now take your seats," she commanded.

Both boys sat down, casting looks of fear and incomprehension at one another. "I will not have disobedience or lateness in my class. Forget that three times and I shall hold you back a grade. You might never leave here," she added with what could only be called a gleam in her eye.

What followed was no less bizarre than what had gone before. The ghost of Miss Hagerman began a lesson on the Civil War. Unfortunately they seemed to have come into the end of a series of classes on this topic, because it wasn't anything to do with juicy battles or cavalry charges, but rather with politics and "reconstruction". With the lateness of the hour and the dullness of the lesson, it wasn't long before Mike and Doug started to doze off.

They awoke to a loud CRACK as the cane was brought down on the desk next to Mike's sleeping head. "No child has ever fallen asleep in my class!" bellowed the teacher. "That will cost you both another caning. Stand and hold out your hands."

Mike looked at Doug and said, "We're out of here," and they both ran for the door.

"Stop!" yelled the ghost, and despite their minds screaming silently inside them that they should not, Mike and Doug felt themselves stop, turn, and walk back to the front of the classroom. "Hands," repeated the ghost.

Feeling like puppets being controlled by somebody else, each boy held out his left hand. WHACK.....WHACK the cane came down, and this time it REALLY hurt. Each boy winced and grimaced as he took his beating, and Mike immediately put his hand to his mouth and sucked on the welt that began to form.

"It's time for lunch. You may go outside, but do not leave the school porch. Douglas, Michael, I see you have your lunch pails on your hooks."

The ghost pointed to a row of hooks along the classroom wall where coats and metal lunch-pails hung. Above each hook was a name. The two closest to the door were labeled "Douglas" and "Michael". Mike and Doug looked at the teacher, and then at each other.

"Too weird," they both mouthed. They picked the lunch pails up by their straps and walked out onto the porch, following the two younger boys. Outside, the porch was lit with ghostly light from no particular source, while all around them was night.

"Dude, what's with your clothes?" Mike asked Doug as they opened their lunchboxes.

"Whadya mean?" replied Doug through a bite of corned beef sandwich. Both boys were stunned to see that the other was wearing a collarless button-down shirt. Doug had on overalls like the younger boys while Mike wore rough woolen pants held up by suspenders..

"This is way too weird, man. We gotta get outta here," said Mike.

"How come it hurt so much more the second time she hit us?" Doug asked.

"She's trapping you," one of the younger boys chimed in.

"Spill it, kid. How did you get here and what the heck is going on?" Mike said.

"I'm Billy and this is Sid. We're Webelos scouts. We came up here one night to check out the lights in the schoolhouse, and Miss Hagerman's ghost caught us just like she caught you."

"Can't you run away either?" asked Mike

"No. We tried, and we couldn't disobey any more than you could. Then she hit us just like she hit you. Have you noticed that she seems more solid now than when you first saw her? We probably look more solid too, don't we? She's pulling you into the ghost world. We're already trapped. She wasn't kidding about three punishments meaning that you never leave. You've already got two strikes. Your clothes have changed. You're more than half way over into the ghost world."

"This is really heavy," said Doug. "How long have you guys been here?"

"We don't know. Day and night are reversed in the ghost world. We appear at the porch to come into school at 9:00 each night and she lets us out at 4:00 each morning. Every day you think you're going to get away, but each time we step off the porch, we just seem to disappear and then we're right back here for another school day."

"Don't you even get weekends?" gasped Doug.

"No. It never ends," said Sid, "and you guys are one punishment away from it now."

Doug and Mike talked about this as they chewed on their "lunches". How were they to get away? If they tried to run they'd be seen, called back, caned, and stuck forever in the ghost school. What if they stayed and worked until the close of the school day? They weren't fully into the ghost world yet. If they could stay out of trouble they might just be able to walk away at 4:00 a.m.

So that was the plan. When the ghost teacher came out and rang the bell for lessons to begin, all four boys trooped inside, Mike shutting the doors *quietly* behind him. Mike and Doug sat down at their desks with straight backs and forced smiles, and waited for instruction from the teacher.

"The Legislature of the Great State of Wisconsin has declared that all children from the ages of six to fourteen shall have the benefit of a public education," began Miss Hagerman. "This school represents the manifestation of that declaration, and you, my students, are its beneficiaries. If you study hard, perhaps you will be able to go to a high school in one of the cities. If not, or if your parents cannot afford further education for you, you will leave here after your eighth grade year and go to work somewhere. Even if they fail the eighth grade, I will not keep older children in my school. You have only one chance, so you, Michael and Douglas, had better make the most of it."

"Yes, Miss Hagerman," replied Doug and Mike in unison.

"Very good" said the teacher, with a note of deep suspicion in her voice.

The afternoon, or should I say, "after midnight", lesson continued. First was mathematics, which was stuff they had done before, and easy. Then came literature. The class was studying *Huckelberry Finn* by Mark Twain, which they had read before. That was no problem. Last in the day was art. Neither of them was any good at drawing, but they struggled to stay awake and focused and really did do their very best work. Miss Hagerman seemed suitably impressed.

At 4:00 a.m. Miss Hagerman announced that the school day was over and that she looked forward to seeing everybody again tomorrow. All four boys walked out of the doors and towards the edge of the porch. Billy reached out a hand to Doug and grasped him by the wrist.

"Take us with you," he begged, almost in tears.

"I don't know if we'll be able to leave ourselves," said Doug, "but it can't hurt to try". So Mike and Doug each took one of the Webelos hands and all four stepped off the porch and out of the light.

Surrounded by darkness now, Mike and Doug immediately reached for the pockets where they kept their flashlights. Thank God, they were back in their proper clothes. The light, however, revealed that they were alone. Sid and Billy, it seemed were condemned to spend the rest of eternity in the ghost classroom.

Our two heroes were very quiet as they returned to their campsite that early morning. They got to their tent and practically fell into their sleeping bags. When the troop bugler sounded off a scratchy reveille at 6:00 the next morning, they crawled out looking like death warmed up, and gathered the other boy-leaders around them to tell their story. The other boys reacted as you would expect. At first they didn't believe it. Then they dared Doug and Mike to prove it to them. Doug and Mike weren't about to go anywhere near Miss Hagerman's schoolhouse again and risk an eternity inside it, so they said, "Fine. Don't believe us. Just don't go up there, okay?"

Saturday's hiking, training and cooking went well, and Mike and Doug felt like maybe they would be able to salvage something of a good time from the weekend. That night, one of the ASMs told a ghost story at campfire. It was kind of lame compared to what they had gone through the previous night, and both Doug and Mike drifted away from the fire and off to bed much earlier than usual. They were awfully tired after only two hours of sleep the night before.

Sometime after midnight, Mike and Doug woke up as they were dumped out of their sleeping bags into the wet grass. Four of the older guys had pulled them out of their tent.

"Let's go check out your ghost school, kiddies," one of them said in a mocking voice. "If your ghost is real we're gonna rescue the little guys. You said that she wouldn't take anyone over fourteen in her school, so we should be safe. If you're lying, we're gonna lock you in there for the rest of the night."

Doug and Mike were terrified. Mike started to shout, but the older guys told him to "man up", and half led, half pushed them along the road and up the hill to the Eckelberry School. Once again, the ghostly light shone from the windows. Mike and Doug begged the older boys not to bring them up to the building, but they wouldn't listen and dragged the two seventh graders up the edge of the porch.

"Okay guys. You two stay outside and we'll go in and get the little guys." The four high-schoolers threw open the doors of the school and strode inside.

When the doors opened, Miss Hagerman looked up sharply and Billy and Sid turned to see who had entered. The young boys' eyes got very big when they saw who stood in the door. Miss Hagerman seemed to grow in intensity and solidity as she strode down the aisle of the classroom towards the stunned older scouts.

"You are too old for my classroom," she bellowed at the older boys.

Her eyes blazed as she raised her hands and made a pinching shape with them in the air. The four older scouts immediately started to gasp for air. Their hands went to their throats as they struggled to breathe and they quickly fell to the floor and started to twitch as they slowly asphyxiated. Doug and Mike watched in horror. They looked at one another and Mike said to Doug, "We have to help them. There's no other choice."

So Mike and Doug jumped up onto the porch and ran into the school. They ignored the intensely angry ghost and grabbed hold of their fellow scouts, dragged them out onto the porch and pushed them off it into the night.

As soon as the high-schoolers rolled off the porch the spell was broken and they were able to breathe again. They picked themselves up and looked at Doug and Mike. The two boys were trying to step off the porch, but couldn't quite seem to do it. The big guys tried to grab hold and pull them off, but Doug and Mike seemed to become thin and the big guys' hands passed right through them rather than grabbing hold. The big guys backed away as they saw that Doug's and Mike's clothes had changed, too. It was just as they had described their experience of the night before.

An evil chuckle sounded behind them, and Doug and Mike turned to see Miss Hagerman standing before them, cane in hand, looking very solid indeed. "Douglas and Michael," she said, "you two boys are late for school".

To this day, the Eckelberry School appears empty and unused by day. If you go up there and peep in at the windows it will seem dirty and disused.

Look at it in the night, though, and you may see a faint glow from the windows. If you get curious, and think that it might be a good idea to look in at the window, you will see four boys toiling away at their lessons in front of a tall teacher in a long dress. If one of them should raise his left hand to answer a question, you might see three ugly stripes across it.

If you are brave enough to look, be sure that you are not seen, and whatever you do, stay off the Eckelberry School porch. Unless you can stay out of trouble, it might be the last time anybody sees you.

10   The Missing Bugler

It had taken Mark a little longer than some to make it to First Class. He had stood with sweaty palms and a worried face under his uncombed blonde hair when the troop OA election had taken place, but it turned out that he had nothing to worry about. Mark was nobody's hero, but he was regarded by the whole troop as a good guy who did his share of the work and could be relied upon to have a deck of cards in his pack on every outing. He was also the troop bugler, and the scouts who were already in the OA thought that having Mark blow signals for the district at Conclaves would be a neat way for them to stand out. After all, going un-noticed is not exactly Troop 628's style.

Now an OA ordeal is no place for a nice scout bugle, so Mark didn't take it on his first OA outing, but the next spring at Camp Indian Trails, he had it with him and put all his heart into the best rendition of *Retreat* that he'd ever played as the colors were retired on Friday evening. At the lodge chief's insistence, he also played *Taps* at lights-out, and dragged himself out of bed at six a.m. on Saturday – that's the worst part of being the bugler, by the way – to squeak your way through *Reveille* with stiff, cold lips.

Saturday was a cool day, so working conditions were good and when the job was done they only had dirt to wash off, rather than sweat *and* dirt as was so often the case. That evening at campfire, the OA dance team performed their newest piece, the

Dance of the Dead. This, their leader explained, is a dance that pays respect to the spirits of chiefs and warriors who have gone on to a glorious afterlife.

Mark woke up early Sunday morning. Judging by the amount of light coming through the tent, he figured it had to be shortly before dawn, but he couldn't get back to sleep, so he grabbed his bugle case and walked through the morning dew to the parade field where he could loosen his lips a bit and play some practice notes in the hope of doing a better job of *Reveille* than on the previous morning.

If you've ever walked around Camp Indian Trails at dawn, you know that in spring and fall there is often a layer of fog over the Rock River that spills into the marshes on the far side, and sometimes even up onto the parade field itself. This was the sight that greeted Mark that Sunday morning as he blew his first wobbly warm-up notes. As musicians often do, he played with his eyes closed, focusing intently on the music, so he was very surprised to open his eyes, look up at the river and see a canoe paddling across from the other side. Squinting through the mist, he was more surprised still to see the shapes of three birch wigwams poking up through the mist on the far side of the river. One man stood in the front of the canoe as another paddled it from the rear. Between the wigwams, a small group of what Mark took to be women and children stood watching the canoe.

As the canoe slid up to the shore on the CIT side, Mark stood and walked down towards the riverbank, bugle in hand. The man in the front of the canoe was dressed in buckskins. His long black hair was tied back in a ponytail with an eagle feather hanging from the clasp. The canoe was of birch bark and both it and the men in it were clearly Native Americans, not scouts dressed up to look like them. The man in the canoe shouted something at Mark and gestured with his arm. Mark didn't understand a word, so he simply shrugged and gave the man the same look he usually gave his social studies teacher. You know – the look you give a teacher when she pulls your attention away from a particularly important daydream with a question about whatever it was that caused you to stop listening and start daydreaming in the first place? Right – that look!

The Indian repeated his shout, but Mark shrugged again and answered in English that he didn't understand. The man frowned and creased his brow in thought. Then he waived to make sure that he had Mark's attention and began a series of gestures that Mark figured were some kind of sign language. Again, Mark shrugged and said that he didn't understand. The man made three quick gestures, then repeated them twice, as if to make sure that Mark understood. Then he turned his back on Mark, leapt back into the canoe, sat down, and joined his comrade in paddling back to the other side.

Mark stood and watched, as if in a trance. When the men reached the other side they didn't turn to look at him. They just went up to the "village", such as it was, and disappeared into a wigwam. Mark snapped out of his daze and ran all the way back to his campsite. It was past time for him to sound *Reveille*, and some of the other guys were already up, so he blew a hasty wake-up call and went straight to the SPL's tent to tell him what he'd seen.

As Mark, the SPL and a few of Mark's friends walked back down to the parade field to confirm Mark's story, Mark went through the final sign-language signs that the Indian had made.

First he ran through them in his mind, then he did them with his hands. They had seemed important, and he didn't want to forget them. It will come as no surprise to you to hear that when they got down to the river the fog was almost gone and there was no sign of people or wigwams. The other guys called Mark a liar and were unhappy to have gotten wet feet, but they didn't chuck him into the river, so it wasn't as bad as it might have been.

They ate quickly, broke camp and headed back home, but Mark kept on running through the signs in his mind all the way home. He practiced the signs on his own in his room, and vowed to find some way to figure out what they meant. He couldn't have imagined it all. He had something real to remember it by.

The school library had nothing useful on Indian sign language and Mark came up with nothing useful on Google either. A trip to the local branch of the public library was more fruitful, however. There, Mark searched the catalog on his own, and came up with endless hits in various branches, but all seemed to be about American Sign Language or Signed English. Who knew that there were different dialects even in sign language for English speakers? Mark spent hours looking through books and videos of signs, but nothing really seemed to match what he had seen the Indian sign to him.

Mark was pretty much out of options and spent several nights fretting about how he was going to figure out the signs. The solution came almost by accident. At the monthly OA meeting, one of the guys on the dance team mentioned that they were going to be having a masterclass from an old Ojibwe who works with them from time to time. He was a folklore specialist who worked with Indian children to teach them the traditions of their people. Maybe *he* could tell Mark what the signs meant.

So Mark went along to the dancers' masterclass. He wasn't part of the dance group so he just hung out against the wall until they took a break. To Mark's surprise, the teacher walked right up to Mark before even going for a drink and asked him why he was there. Mark took a deep breath and asked point-blank if the teacher could tell him what some Indian signs meant. The guy said that he'd try, so Mark carefully signed the phrase exactly as he remembered it. The reaction was not at all what he expected. The teacher gave a big grin, clapped Mark on the shoulder and then started laughing.

"What?" Mark asked. "What does it mean?"

"It means," said the Indian, "it means 'You are too stupid to talk to.'" And then he laughed again and asked who had taught Mark the sign.

Mark didn't know what to say, so he asked how he should answer. The teacher thought for a while and then said, "How about, 'I am not as stupid as you think!'"

Mark thought that was pretty good, so the teacher showed him how to sign that. Mark practiced it a couple of times and then he had it down. Of course, he knew the sign for "stupid" already!

"Do you want to learn some more?" the old Indian asked.

"Yes!" The reply was out of Mark's mouth almost immediately.

"Write down my name and do a library search on it," the teacher said. "I made VHS tapes of all the basics years ago so that the Ojibwe kids I teach could work on it at home. Get a set through interlibrary loan. If you think you're making good progress and want to learn more, get your parent's permission and my phone number from the scout office. I can do a couple of classes for you if you like."

"Really?" Mark asked.

"Sure, I'm retired. All I do now is teach the young ones the old ways. I teach these guys our dance, why shouldn't I teach you our sign language?"

It took two long weeks for the videos to arrive, and then Mark had to buy a VHS player from a guy selling one on Craig's list to be able to play them. He probably studied the sign language a bit too hard. Several assignments at school got missed or turned in late, and both his teachers and his parents started to get on his case about it. In quiet moments, or during boring classes, he would practice the signs, having little conversations with himself. Mark's friends at school and his big brother began to think that he was more than a little weird. Mark, however, was determined that if he saw the Indian in the fog at CIT a second time, he would be prepared.

The Council's next OA weekend was scheduled for August at EBSR, but it got shifted to CIT a week before-hand because logging operations at EBSR ran later than planned. Once again Mark took his bugle and played for the ceremonies as needed. Once again, the OA dancers danced the *Dance of the Dead*.

That night, Mark hardly slept at all. He couldn't wait for the first rays of dawn. Dawn came soon enough, however, and he took his bugle in his hand and walked softly through the grass to the parade field. As usual, the Rock River was hidden by a layer of fog, but there was no sign of the wigwams or the canoe from the spring. Disappointed, Mark sat down on the dock and blew a few clear notes on his bugle just to warm up his lips.

When he looked up, there again was the canoe in the fog. This time it almost flew through the water as both men propelled it across the river. Both men were in their prime. Mark guessed that the guy in the front of the canoe was about nineteen and the guy in the back a year or two older. The man in front had more beads on his clothes and was obviously in charge, however.

When he leapt onto the dock he strode straight up to Mark and yelled something at Mark in his own tongue. Mark gave him a blank look, just like last time, and the Indian again signed, "You are too stupid to talk to," then turned his back on Mark.

Mark wasn't going to miss the opportunity he'd worked so hard for, however. He said, "Turn around," loudly enough that the Indian stopped and turned to scowl at him. "I am not as stupid as you think," Mark signed.

The Indian gave a surprised look and signed, "Why did you awaken us?"

"Wake you? How?" Mark signed back.

"You do the *Dance of the Dead* and then you blow a horn at dawn. You have called back the spirits of the fallen people. You are not of the Blackhawk. Why do you call us?"

Mark was stunned. "I didn't know we had," he said out loud.

"I do not understand your words," the Indian signed back. So Mark signed, as best he could, "We did not mean to."

"We have Council," the Indian signed, and he motioned for Mark to get into the canoe. Mark wasn't so sure about that, but the Indian gripped Mark's bicep in his hand and led him to the end of the dock and into the middle of the big canoe. The guy was so much bigger than Mark that there didn't seem to be any point in resisting, and he hadn't reached for either the tomahawk or the knife at his waist, so Mark didn't fear for his safety. Well, not much anyway.

They seemed to cross the river in no time. Mark was led up to the door of the largest wigwam as the people of the small village watched in fascination. The big Indian propelled him inside. Mark's eyes immediately began to sting from the wood smoke that filled the wigwam as it rose from the fire in the center to the hole in the roof. The men from the canoe shoved Mark down to sit next to the fire, then sat down on either side of him. As Mark's eyes adjusted to the smoke and the dim light, he made out the shapes of three other Indians, all older, around the fire. The big Indian spoke briefly, then the oldest man signed, "What tribe are you?"

Mark signed back, "I am a scout."

"Your tribe, not your job," replied the old man.

Mark thought for a moment, then signed, "It is changed. All my people are scouts. We call ourselves the Scout tribe." It wasn't exactly correct, but he was effectively trying to speak a foreign language that he'd learned from video-tape. Could you do any better!?

The Indians discussed that for a minute then one of the other elders signed, "Where did your tribe learn our dance?"

That was much easier for Mark to answer. He had planned how to say that because he thought that the question would be asked. "From an elder. He teaches young ones who will learn." The three older men seemed to like that answer. They smiled at each other and nodded.

Then came the question Mark was dreading. "Why did you call us, the honored dead, from our sleep?"

"We dance to honor you," he signed. "The call was not for you. It was just a boy blowing a horn. I did not know." Mark hung his head for a moment, then looked up to see the Indians exchanging glances of disbelief.

"Today you knew that you called us," the oldest man signed. It was a statement, not a question.

"I wanted to talk to you," Mark signed.

The old man smiled. "Speak," he signed.

This was one step farther than Mark had planned. He didn't really know what he wanted to ask them. The plan had only been to see if he could communicate with them. Obliged to wing it now, Mark signed, "How did you gain honor?"

The old man nodded and smiled at Mark. "Wisdom and leadership," he signed, then looked at the man to his right.

"Battle," was the next sign.

"Skill with the bow," signed the older of the two from the canoe.

"Battle," signed the younger.

The last man's sign was not one that Mark knew. Seeing that Mark did not understand, the man mimed grabbing the nineteen year-old by the neck and shaking him, then stopped and made the sign for no. All the Indians roared with laughter and Mark laughed along with them. "Patience," of course.

When the laughter died down, the patient one signed to Mark, "You are not yet a man. How will you win honor?"

All eyes in the room seem to bore into Mark as he considered his answer and how to sign it. Mark took a good quarter of a minute before he answered. "I will be the best scout I can," he signed, "and I will do as I must."

"It is a good answer, young one," the man signed back.

Quite suddenly, the oldest Indian stood up and it was clear that the council was over. Before he left the wigwam, he looked hard at Mark and signed, "You may visit us again. If you earn a name, you must tell us."

The Indians left the wigwam one by one, in order of age. Mark followed them out into the sunshine. The two men from the canoe started down to the water's edge and Mark made to follow them, but his way was blocked by all the women and children of the village. They crowded round and touched his clothes and his hair. One of the women even pulled a couple blonde strands out and held them up for the others to see. That hurt, so Mark pushed through and followed the young Indian men down to the canoe.

Once again they paddled him across the river with astonishing speed. Mark watched their stroke and silently vowed to learn to paddle like that before he met them again. As Mark climbed up onto the dock, the younger Indian in the canoe pointed to his breast and said some words. Then he made the sign for "running buffalo" and again pointed to himself. Then he pointed to Mark with a questioning look. All Mark could do was to say his name in return. Running Buffalo signed, "What does it mean?"

"Nothing," was all Mark could sign in reply.

Running Buffalo pointed at Mark with his paddle, then signed, "No name is no man. Goodbye, boy," and with that they paddled away. The canoe and the village seemed to fade away into the mist at the same time as the canoe crossed back over the river.

It was a full year before the OA returned to CIT to camp. As boys of around thirteen will, Mark changed a lot. He put on three inches and twelve pounds. Most of it was muscle and bone. He was good to his promise to learn to canoe better and even bought some free weights with his Christmas money so that he could work his upper body muscles during the winter months.

He convinced his dad to let him work on his signing with the old Ojibwe teacher. Mark was an able student, and both he and the old man looked forward to the visits. Mark's dad would drive him up to Black River Falls once a month. His dad was a scouter, and the time alone in the car was a good opportunity for them to talk about scouts without Mark's mom rolling her eyes, or about anything else that was on either of their minds.

Mark had also thought about what Running Buffalo had said about earning a name for himself. He had asked the other scouts for ideas but nobody would take him seriously. "Needs a

Haircut" and "Foul Breath" were not the sort of suggestions he could really do anything with.

Summer camp that year, however, gave him a name without him even looking for it. At the end of one particularly hot day he had taken his patrol down to the lake to fish. One of the little guys had managed to hook the biggest northern pike Mark had ever seen. He fought the thing for about ten minutes and wasn't getting anywhere near getting it in, so he asked Mark for help and Mark played it like a pro for twenty minutes more until he was able to give the rod back to the first year who just reeled it in. After that, Mark was dubbed "the fish fighter", so he figured out the signs and was ready to meet Running Buffalo again.

Mark spent every spare moment of that summer at the library or on the internet reading and learning everything he could about the Native peoples of Wisconsin. The more he read, the more he "got into" the whole Native American way of life. He grew his hair out, not knowing what a "proper" hairstyle would be, but knowing that it would need to be long. He tried to learn the Blackhawk and Ojibwe words for common things. He talked his parents into taking him to dance festivals. He ordered buckskin and a leather sewing kit online and worked with his mom to make a pair of buckskin pants and a shirt. He even dealt with being the only boy in a beading class at Joanne Fabrics so that he could learn how to adorn his new clothing properly.

Mark also joined the OA Native American Dance group, and began to learn the steps of the grass dances and the *Dance of the Dead*. As August approached, Mark was horrified to find that the dance group was not planning to do the *Dance of the Dead* at campfire. How was he supposed to join the Blackhawk council if the honored dead were not summoned by the dance? He pleaded and pleaded with the leaders of the dance group until they almost threw him out because he was acting so weird. In the end, he resolved to simply do the *Dance of the Dead* himself. It might be enough. It would *have* to be enough.

At last, the end of August arrived and Mark was as ready as he could be. He offered to be fire warden on Friday night when everyone else said that they were ready for bed. He stayed up with the dying fire, and when all was quiet in camp, he began the *Dance of the Dead*, quietly chanting the cadence of the words as he hopped and twisted around the fire. When the dance was complete, he stood panting by the fire until he cooled down a little. Then he doused it with the fire bucket and slipped into his tent.

Mark had arranged a tent to himself for that night. He set his alarm for 5:00, and when it rang, he fished his buckskins out of his pack and got dressed in his full Native American gear. He tied a magpie feather into a bandana and tied that around his head, then took his bugle under his arm and began to walk down to the parade field.

The sky was bright. Above the valley, the sun was probably already shining but down on the edge of the river it would be another forty-five minutes before the sun rose high enough to chase the fog off the river. There was no sign of the Blackhawk village on the far bank. Mark could feel his heart pounding in his chest. In his soul he knew that it would work, but his head told him that this time was different. Only he had danced the dance, not the full dance group.

Mark walked out onto the beach, licked his lips, closed his eyes, raised the bugle and blew a single clear, crisp note. When he opened his eyes the sight that he saw brought a huge smile to his face. The wigwams were there, there was smoke rising from the fires, and Running Buffalo was standing in the front of his canoe, already half way across the river, waving. Mark set the bugle down by some driftwood and walked out to meet Running Buffalo.

Running Buffalo looked him up and down with a broad smile. "You have grown. You look good," he signed. "What shall I call you?"

"Fish Fighter," Mark replied in his best Blackhawk. Then he signed it as well, just in case he had blown the pronunciation. Running Buffalo grasped him by both shoulders and pointed to the canoe. Mark stepped in and saw that the man in the back was also smiling.

"I am called Coyote," he said, making the sign for coyote as he spoke the word.

"Coyote," Mark repeated and was rewarded with a friendly laugh.

The welcome was equally warm in the village. Again, the women and children fussed over him as he walked through the group. But this time some of the teenage girls were very much at the front and giggling among themselves. In the wigwam, the old men too seemed pleased with Mark. He was able to understand some of what was said and he mixed words with his signs when he knew them.

They had been in the Council Circle in the wigwam for almost an hour when the oldest of the elders (who had since introduced himself as War Hammer) looked him directly in the eye and said, "You have become much like us. Why do you do this?"

Mark could not break away from his gaze. He thought about his answer for a long time before replying. The more time and effort he had put into his Indian obsession, the less time he had spent with his friends and family. It seemed to Mark that he wasn't really part of his old, modern life any more. It was the young Blackhawk man growing inside him who defined who he was now. He felt more like Fish Fighter than Mark. Looking War Hammer straight in the eye, he said/signed, "I feel as though I belong here more than I belong with my own people."

War Hammer thought about this for a long time. "Would you stay with us, if you could?" he asked. "If you stay, you will be one of the honored dead, but you will never die. You will live forever, but only know life when you are called. Is this what you want?"

Running Buffalo nudged Mark and nodded at him, encouraging him to say yes. Mark tried to think of why he would make the decision one way or the other, but it was all too confusing to think through. All at once, he made up his mind. "Yes," Mark said in Blackhawk.

"Let us paddle!" Running Buffalo said. He jumped up and led Mark out of the wigwam and down to the river. They climbed into the canoe, pushed off, and dug deeply into the water with their paddles. The two of them flew up and down the river. Like a knife, they sliced through the fog. Both Mark and Running Buffalo put their full force into paddling. Mark had never felt so happy or as completely alive as he did at that moment on the Rock River when he faded into the fog.

Mark's bugle was found at 8:30 that morning. The OA got nothing done in the way of service work that day. The whole time was spent combing every inch of the camp for Mark. On Sunday, the police, the county sheriff dive squad and half the adult scouters in the council turned out as well, but the only evidence of Mark was his empty tent, the bugle, and a set of size nine moccasin prints on the far shore.

Since his first meeting with the Blackhawk eighteen months before, Mark had not spoken of them to anyone except his dad. Even those conversations had been guarded because, let's face it, it was pretty hard to believe. In the end, Mark's dad couldn't deal with the thought that his son was dead, and fixed on his having taken his Native American obsession to some bizarre extreme.

Each time the OA meets at Camp Indian Trails, you will find Mark's dad in the parade field at dawn with Mark's bugle. He doesn't know about the *Dance of the Dead*, he just blows a few notes on the bugle at dawn and hopes for a glimpse of his son. If you ask him, he'll swear that one time he saw two Indians paddle swiftly past in a canoe, and that one of them was a young man with blonde hair tied back in a ponytail who looked very much like his son. Everyone says that that's just the imagination of a man who won't give up on his son. But still he comes, each time the OA meets at CIT, waiting at dawn, hoping for a glimpse of the Missing Bugler.

11 How Gordie Came to Castle Rock

Some of you may know that Ranger Gordie has been in charge of EBSR, or Camp Castle Rock as it was known then, since 1983. Gordie is a bit of a legend in his own time, and few people remember his predecessor. Even fewer know how the job came to be open, and fewer still speak of the events that led up to it.

It all started on a beautiful, clear night just like tonight. It was the second week of summer camp. The camp staff had made it through the first week with its inspections, mistakes, equipment shortages and all the little unexpected problems that go along with the first week of camp. The ranger, Bob Farrar, and that summer's camp director were pleased with how things were going.

It was already the third night of that week's camp, and Bob was making the rounds of the troop campfires, listening to lots of stories he'd heard before and one or two jokes and skits that were new. At Comanche camp, he sat with Troop 53 from Lincolnwood, IL. It was a small troop, only 9 boys and a couple of adults, but the boys were creative and having a good time. Troop 53 only had one new scout that year, a kid named Sammy Pedzinski, four feet six inches tall, with blonde hair that went with his Polish heritage, a goofy grin and an infectious laugh that he couldn't contain as the older boys entertained.

Bob sat across from Sammy at the fire, and took special note of how happy he seemed. Yes, it was a good week at camp.

Bob went back to the ranger's cabin after Taps and turned in for the night. He was awakened the next morning by a loud hammering on his door and the sound of distant emergency sirens. The staff member who woke him was in a terrible panic and wasn't really making much sense, but "ripped tent" and "blood everywhere" were definitely in there. Bob dragged the counselor to his truck, shoved the boy into the passenger seat, jumped behind the wheel, fired it up and spun the wheels as he blew out of the driveway and down the dirt road into the camp. "Where?" he yelled at the counselor.

"C-C-C-Comanche," the counselor managed to stammer.

"The farthest camp, it just had to be!" thought Bob, and he threw the wheel left, going round against his own "One Way" signs to get there as fast as he could. Grabbing his walkie-talkie, Bob called for any staffer and told the first person who answered to direct the emergency vehicles to Comanche as soon as they arrived.

Pulling into Comanche camp, Bob found eight boys huddled together around a picnic table with an assistant scoutmaster. A couple of the younger ones were in tears and the older ones were pale and obviously in a state of shock. Half way up the hill, the scoutmaster stood with a staff member, looking at the remains of a Timberline tent, its ripped rain fly flapping in the morning breeze. The ridge-pole was snapped and the two "A"s of the frame had fallen in towards the middle.

Bob jogged over to the tent, taking in the situation as he approached and cursing the ache that seemed to be coming from the side of his head. He'd missed his morning coffee. "What's happened?" he demanded of the two men standing over the tent.

"It's Sammy Pedzinski," said the scoutmaster. "He's disappeared, and look at what's left of his tent."

Look at the tent?! Bob could barely drag his eyes off it. The inner tent fabric was soaked with blood and the left walls of the tent and fly were slashed from the rear apex to the middle of the floor. It was as if someone, or some*thing,* had sliced through it with four sharp knives, all at the same time, leaving the fabric in three perfect ribbons between the cuts.

"Back away carefully. The sheriff's going want to secure this area as a crime scene," Bob told the scoutmaster and the counselor. The three of them walked carefully away from the tent, and then a terrible thought struck Bob. "Where's his buddy?" he demanded of the scoutmaster.

"He didn't have one," the scoutmaster replied.

"You let a Tenderfoot scout sleep alone?" Bob asked him, not really expecting an answer. Bob had served in the Marines in Vietnam, and the look he gave the scoutmaster was the sort that drill instructors reserve for the most pathetic recruit. The scoutmaster seemed to shrink by about a foot and looked like he wanted to crawl into one of his own boots and hide.

Bob got on his radio. The Juneau County Sheriff arrived first, followed by an ambulance, a couple of deputies and then one state trooper after another. The scouts in camp were gathered in the YBR and on the parade field with some leaders. The mood was quiet and somber. A lot of boys called home from the pay-phone in the YBR and asked their parents to come and take them home. The camp staff and all but one adult from each group were organized into search parties and spent the rest of the day searching the camp, but there was no trace of Sammy Pedzinski.

At four o'clock, as everyone was getting hungry and in need of a break, the sheriff called across the radio for all searchers to return to the YBR to report in and get some food and fresh water. Each party in turn gave its report. Most had nothing to tell, but as the deputies who had gathered evidence in Comanche Camp gave their report you could have heard a pin drop over the silence of all who listened to their story. They told of bloody footprints found leading up to and away from Sammy's tent. The footprints were bigger than a man's, and squarer; not human, that was for sure. At the camp road, the footprints stopped, and all that could be seen were the tire tracks from where Bob's truck and all the police vehicles had come blazing in that morning.

As soon as the deputies finished their report everybody in the room started talking. "Why did bloody prints lead *to* and *from* the tent?" "What could it mean?" "Who could it be?"

Only one person in the room remained silent. David Red Cloud, a young man of the Black River Ojibwa who had been hired to teach woodcraft and Indian Lore that summer, had turned white as a sheet. He got up slowly and walked through the crowd to the pay phone. There, he took a quarter out of his pocket, very deliberately pushed it into the slot, and dialed a seven digit number. As he listened to the phone ring, David realized that the room had gone quiet. All eyes were on him as he said very deliberately and clearly, "Uncle? It's Red Cloud. There's a Windigo at the scout camp."

David Red Cloud hung up the phone and looked at the faces turned toward him. "My uncle, Paul Running Bear, is a medicine man. He will find out what has happened. He will know what to do."

"What the H&!! is a Windigo?" the sheriff demanded. "What do you know son?"

But David Red Cloud would not explain. No matter who asked him, he only repeated, "My uncle will come. He will look. He will explain."

A little less than an hour later a slightly rusted green Ford Fairmont rolled into the camp and stopped in front of the YBR. A man of about fifty got out. He was dressed mostly in the manner of your typical American, but he wore a bone and bead choker which together with his long black hair and swarthy skin marked him as a Native American. He walked up to the sheriff and David Red Cloud and shook hands with the sheriff. "Show me," he said simply.

Now, the sheriff was more than a little ticked off to find his investigation suddenly in the hands of a couple of Indians. He was supposed to be in charge, after all. But he also had a missing kid, a blood covered tent, no good leads, and these people seemed to know something. Something being better than nothing, he decided to hold his tongue and run with it. The sheriff started towards his car but Paul Running Bear said, "No, we walk. I can't track anything inside a car."

So the two Indians and the sheriff set off across the Ridge Trail for Comanche camp. Paul Running Bear looked left and right, up into the trees and down among the wood chips on the path as they walked. His lips were still but his eyes were in constant motion as he took in every twig and blade of grass around him. Entering Comanche camp from the trail he stopped and looked around. "It looks like a herd of Buffalo came through here," he said. "This is not going to be easy."

Shaking his head slightly at the foolishness of those who had so disturbed the evidence before he could see it, Paul Running Bear picked his way, step by step, down into Comanche Camp.

Though much had been trampled, the tent was still as it had been found, and care had been taken not to disturb the footprints. The medicine man studied the footprints carefully, then followed them as they led between the road and the camp. As I have told you, Paul Running Bear's eyes looked up as well as down, and in those days there were many more trees, alive and dead, here in camp. As he walked towards the road, he stopped and pointed up at a broken branch on one of the trees. "What do you think?" he asked David Red Cloud. "Eleven feet up, maybe twelve?"

David nodded, "About that, yes."

"Hmm..." the old Indian replied, and kept on walking. Paul Running Bear ended his search by looking closely at the tent. He measured the three ribbons of nylon where it had been cut, and he finished by crawling around on the ground, smelling the bloody footprints, and finally having a long sniff in one spot about 15 feet behind the remains of Sammy's tent. "Here. Here is where the boy was when he first saw him," he said.

"We can drive back. Call one of your deputies," declared Paul Running Bear. So the sheriff radioed for a squad car and in three minutes they were all back at the YBR.

"Gather all who will remain in camp at the campfire bowl," Running Bear ordered, then he stepped over to the phone, shoved in a quarter and barked a few words of Ojibwa into the receiver before hanging up. With the increasingly irritated sheriff and his deputies behind him, followed closely by the remaining scouts, adults and camp staff, Paul Running Bear strode down to the campfire bowl. Once all were seated, Running Bear rose and faced his audience.

"My nephew thinks there is a Windigo in your camp. He is right!" began Running Bear. "Sheriff, do you know what 'Windigo' is?"

"No Paul. Why don't you enlighten us?" replied the sheriff, his anger clear in his voice.

"For all your learning, your radios, your computers and your cameras, there are things in the Northwoods that the white-man will never understand. The red man has been here for a thousand winters, and he knows. In every legend there is a grain of truth, and if you listen to the stories of your elders you may learn things that the television and even the books in your library may never teach you.

"A Windigo is an evil spirit, and it is also a man. The Windigo is tortured by a desire to eat human flesh. He does not want to kill, but he needs to eat. Windigo is a shape shifter. He can appear as the man he once was, and when he does he is unaware that he is also Windigo, but his heart is a chunk of ice and he knows no compassion. When he changes to his 'monster' form

I suppose you would call it, he becomes twice his normal height. His fingers and toes turn to razor sharp claws, his teeth to points and his body becomes covered with shaggy hair. You have heard the legends of Sasquatch in the northwestern forests? There are some among the Ojibwa and the Cree of these northern forests who say that Sasquatch is a Windigo, but we will never know unless one is caught. Windigo can make himself invisible, but when he does, he leaves a footprint of his own blood on the ground where he steps.

"Now you may think this creature to be a terrible, bellowing or howling monster, but his cry is more terrible by far than any roar. Windigo makes only a hiss; a rustling hiss, like a gentle wind in the leaves. It is a sound that chills the spine of the bravest warrior who walks alone at night, for the Indian knows that Windigo hunts only at night, and he hunts only those who walk alone.

"What happened to your scout is this. He got up from his tent in the night and walked behind it to pee. I smelled the spot where he went. As he relieved himself, he saw or heard the Windigo at the road, but the creature made himself invisible. Clearly, your scout knew that he was in danger because he ran back to his tent and crawled inside thinking that in his tent he would find some measure of safety, but no. Just as surely as a raccoon or a skunk can cut through a tent wall in search of candy, so it offers no protection from a twelve foot tall monster with six inch long claws. The sleeping bag was not cut. The poor boy did not even make it into his bed before he was taken. Windigo carried him off to the road, and there he made himself visible again, and his trail is lost."

There was a long hush. Finally it was broken by Sammy's scoutmaster. "How do we find this Windigo, and how do we kill it?" he asked, an edge of steel in his voice.

"A man becomes a Windigo because he has tasted human flesh," replied Paul Running Bear. "To eat the body of another man is a cold, cold act, and it is this that turns his heart to ice. To kill a Windigo, you must cut open his body, cut out his heart of ice, cut it up with an axe, and burn it in a fire. Only then is the Windigo dead, and the spirit of the man he once was is able to go free.

"In the old days, when we had to hunt for food and live on our crops saved from summer to get through the winter, the braves of our people would sometimes find themselves at starvation's edge while on a hunting party in winter. Then, there was more trouble with Windigo. Now, we buy our food in the grocery store. Men are not starving. They do not need to eat their brothers to survive the cold and hunger. I have not known of a Windigo while I have been alive, though sometimes when I see on the news that someone has disappeared in the Northwoods and the body is never found, I wonder.

"There is a second way that a man can become Windigo. The Windigo's bite is like that of the werewolf of European legends. To be bitten by the Windigo and survive is to share his curse."

"But you know of a Windigo now, and you know who he is, don't you?" shouted the Scoutmaster. "Is it one of your people? Tell me!" The scoutmaster was on his feet now, a wicked looking eight inch sheath knife glinting in his hand. (Those were the days before the Council Safety Committee banned us from carrying fixed blades in camp.)

"I do not know, but I suspect. It is a man who bears a bruise on his head from where he hit it on the branch of a tree," said Running Bear. "And he is not one of my people. He is one of yours."

The hush that came over the assembly was incredible. Every man and boy in the campfire bowl could feel his heart beating in his chest. Everyone but one man. One man who suddenly realized that he could *not* feel his heart beating. In that instant Bob Farrar felt himself being grabbed by four pairs of dark skinned hands. A rage and a hunger grew in him. Even as he grew he remembered how he had wondered. What would it taste like? Was it really 'just like chicken'? The F4s that had napalmed the NVA position his platoon was trying to take in Vietnam had cooked the enemy very nicely. The corpse of the man before him was charred on the outside. He reached down and tore a piece of tricep off the man's arm. Yeah, just like chicken.

Bob snapped out of his flashback to see his hairy body writhing to get free of the hands that held it. He was bigger than these men and boys, and he wanted to feast on them but they were so many and they were binding his hands and legs as he struggled. He tried making himself invisible, but it was no good; the knots that bound him were secure.

His nose told him that a fire was being lit behind him, and the last thing Bob's eyes saw as he gave up the struggle and changed back into his man's shape was the scoutmaster's knife as it plunged down into his chest.

The scouts and men in the campfire bowl that night cut out Bob Farrar's icy heart. They chopped it up with an axe, and they burned it in the ceremonial fire pit. When the deed was done, medicine man Paul Running Bear stood before them again. "All of you now understand something of the ways of the Indian. Do you think you could explain it to judge and jury in words? Could you explain what happened here tonight on CNN?"

At Running Bear's suggestion, all those present swore that they would stick to the story that Bob Farrar too had disappeared the previous night. His body was buried beneath the fire-pit in Comanche camp, and his fate would be forever linked to that of poor Sammy Pedzinski.

Most of the people in camp on that July day so may years ago kept the secret, but a few have let it be told. Gordie was hired to fill the vacancy created by Bob's (cough) disappearance, and to this day, each night before Taps, Gordie drives the camp road and looks into the woods and into the camps. And to this day, the camp commissioners walk the trails of camp after dark, showing scouts the way back to their camps.

But you see, 21st-century boy scouts who wander alone are not the only thing they look for. Sammy Pedzinski's body was never found. They don't know if he was killed and devoured by the Windigo, or whether he was only injured and bitten, to fall under its curse. On quiet nights such as this when the wind hisses through the trees of Camp Castle Rock, Gordie and his camp commissioners are out there looking for the figure of a boy scout in a 1983 uniform, or a shape in the darkness who stands nine feet tall. And to this day, scouts are reminded that they should always have a buddy while in camp, even when they go out to pee in the night.

Glossary

APL

Assistant Patrol Leader. Patrols consist of six to ten scouts and are led by an elected Patrol Leader and his assistant.

Arrowmen

Members of the Order of the Arrow (OA) – see later entry in this glossary

ASM

Assistant Scoutmaster. ASMs back up the scoutmaster (SM) in leading a scout troop on outings and activities. They may fill the role of SM if the SM himself can't go on an outing, or simply help with driving, logistics, supervision and entertainment.

B, Mrs.

Mrs. B. is the Summer Camp Director at Ed Bryant Scout Reservation. She is also a former scoutmaster of Troop 628, a good sport, and has forgotten more about teaching boys than most of us will ever learn.

CC

The troop committee chair – he or she runs meetings of the adult troop committee who provide support to the Scoutmasters, look after administration, make sure that the troop budget is balanced, etc.

CIT

Camp Indian Trails is one of three camp properties owned by the Glacier's Edge Council. It is located on the Rock River a few miles north of Janesville, WI. A deep ravine runs through the center of the camp. A tall and somewhat rickety bridge connects the campsites on the southern end of the camp to Allen Hall (the dining and kitchen facility) and the northern end of the camp.

Cracker Barrel

Snacks before going to bed. A typical evening at a weekend scout outing ends with Cracker Barrel consisting of cookies and/or crackers, cheese and summer sausage. Leaders who are deer hunters often bring venison sausage to share.

Cyrus, Miley

A teen girl pop singer and TV actress, beloved of pre-teen girls at the time this story was written (~2010). Having Miley Cyrus posters in his room would be <u>really</u> embarrassing for a middle-school age boy.

Devil's Lake

Devil's Lake is the center-piece of Devil's Lake State Park, just south of Baraboo, WI. It is deep, clear and cold.

EBSR

Ed Bryant Scout Reservation (near Mauston, WI). Formerly called Camp Castle Rock. This is where the Glacier's Edge Council runs its largest scout summer camp program.

OA – Order of the Arrow

The OA is an honor society within scouting. Unusually, its members are elected by non-members, based on who they consider to be people who they find to be examples of leadership and cheerful service. OA members gather twice per year to give volunteer labor in whatever way is needed to make repairs or improvements at the three camps of the Glacier's Edge Council.

Patrol Leader

Patrols consist of six to ten scouts and are led by an elected Patrol Leader and his assistant.

Scout Executive

The senior professional in the local "Council" of the Boy Scouts of America.

SPL

Senior Patrol Leader. The SPL is the senior youth leader in a scout troop. Not necessarily the oldest in the group, but usually one of the older boys, he is elected by the scouts and typically serves in this position for 1 year.

YBR

The Yellow Band Room, or YBR was the mess hall in Camp Castle Rock prior to the construction of the Fellowship Hall with funds from a bequest from the estate of Ed Bryant. It was the largest indoor space in the camp at the time.

Webelos

These are the oldest group of cub scouts. They are 4th and 5th graders who will *cross over* into boy scouts in February or March of their 5th grade year at the age of 10 or 11. Webelos is a contraction of "We'll be loyal scouts"

Woodman Center

A scout camp property in a valley north of Richland Center, WI. The Woodman Center is part of the range of a pack of coyotes who will howl back to you if you can do a do a good imitation of a coyote howl on a quiet night.

ABOUT THE AUTHOR

Gordon Bain grew up on the outskirts of Stirling, Scotland. He was never in scouts as a boy but is making up for that omission as an adult. He first volunteered as a scout leader in 2003 when his son joined Cub Scouts and has served as an Assistant Den Leader, Assistant Cubmaster, Cubmaster, Cub Scout Leader Trainer and Assistant Scoutmaster with the Boy Scouts of America. He resides in Verona, Wisconsin, with his wife and two children.

In his current role in Scouting, Bain serves as Outings Coordinator, Dutch oven cooking instructor and storyteller for Troop 628.

Made in the USA
Lexington, KY
14 February 2017